Asher Brock's last summer of youth is far from ideal. His hopes for the future, including an escape from his constricting Ozark Mountains hometown, seem increasingly fragile as he faces hurdles of poverty and abuse, all while coming to terms with being gay. Raised by an alcoholic single mother, he clings to his noted intelligence as an escape to a better life. But it will take more than brains—namely, strength of character and aspiration—for him to navigate the months leading to his senior year of high school.

The pregnancy of his recent girlfriend, the heightened aggression of his long-time bully, and the increasing presence of his long-absent father create a season of turmoil, spurring unease and self-doubt. But with support from family and friends, an opportunity for love, and the shedding of generations of secrets, Asher sees beyond preordained fate and starts to realize the opportunities in his grasp.

SUMMER'S SECOND

JEFF BILLINGTON

A NineStar Press Publication

www.ninestarpress.com

Summer's Second

First Edition, December 2022

ISBN: 978-1-64890-592-6

Also available in eBook, ISBN: 978-1-64890-591-9

CONTENT WARNING:

This book contains depictions of alcohol use/addiction, smoking,
bullying, graphic violence, homophobic language, incest, miscarriage, and mentions of past rape and pedophilia.

For my dearest Caio, for forgiving me for using my time to write instead of learning Portuguese.

To Brandan.
Thank you for wanting
a copy & being a friend for
my beautiful niece.

Jill B.

CHAPTER ONE

ASHER'S NOSE WRINKLED and his mouth sagged into a frown as the acrid stench of cigarette smoke and cheap vodka greeted him. A comingled foulness with a source that needed little investigation, as left in an untidy manner on the coffee table were his mother's cracked plastic ashtray and an empty bottle of vodka—the remnants of her previous evening's activities. A disheartened sigh escaped him. *At least she practiced consistency,* with the only variation to note this morning being the absence of a glass, which had probably made its way to her bedroom so she could finish it off as a nightcap.

He picked up the vodka bottle and peered into its bottom, drained to the last few drops. The ashtray was the opposite, overflowing with twisted butts and ash. He carried the pair of containers into the kitchen and set them on the counter. Finishing cleaning the mess now made the most sense, but doing so in his current mood would leave him seething with frustration. That could wait, he told himself, and returned to the living room. He collapsed onto the sofa, a loud sigh escaping as he did so, then reached across to the coffee table, straightening the pile of months-old fashion magazines, souvenirs from the recycling at his mother's HairStylez job, then wiping the lingering ashes and water spots off the table.

The night before, as always, he left the room tidy. Disorder made him uneasy. But, also as usual, after an evening at the bar, any notion his mother had of good housekeeping vanished once she stretched out on the sofa with her smokes and cocktail, ready to enjoy her recording of that day's episode of *General Hospital.* Sometime around midnight, she likely staggered off to bed, obliviously leaving behind the mess. There she contently dozed away the next eight hours until her alarm woke her for another day of providing cheap haircuts. He hoped that, as she passed through the living room on the way to her car, she paused a moment at the mess from the night before and felt a pang of guilt for leaving it to her son to clean.

The thought of the bottle and ashtray on the counter gnawed at him, appealing to his growing compulsion for cleanliness, so he pushed back to his feet and returned to the kitchen. Being careful not to tip out any of its waste, he lifted the ashtray to eye level, examining the twisted and charred cigarette filters, ensuring no red glow remained and he could safely dump the remnants into the trash can. After nine hours, they were always burned out, but his overabundant sense of caution insisted he verify each morning. The overwhelming scent of burnt menthol clogged his nose, giving his stomach a start. How could an odor he had known every day of his life, which all but permeated his home, nearly prompt him to puke?

He dropped the vodka bottle into the trash can, glass clinking as it hit against an identical bottle emptied three days prior. Another exasperated sigh escaped him as he pushed the trash can against the kitchen cabinet, so he could brush a handful of stale potato chips and a puddle of pickle juice into it—the last of the mess she'd left.

The immediate disorder now abated, Asher felt enough ease to return to the sofa for a little TV time, his morning relaxation before heading to his summer job of bussing tables and washing dishes at the diner.

A collection of annoyingly gleeful faces appeared on the screen, clueless morning program personalities bobbing their heads up and down in affirmation of the segment's slick promotional guests. It felt so fake. How could anyone act so endlessly excited unless they were popping pills or snorting coke in their dressing rooms? He had never done either pills or coke so he could only assume the effect of those drugs mirrored the idiocy he saw on the television. He slid his hand up and down the left side of the sofa cushion, finding nothing, then leaned over to the right side and dug in, snagging the remote from its hiding place. His mother always seemed to misplace it following her nightly soap opera viewing parties. He punched in the number for the classic movie channel, and the iconic face of James Dean appeared, a troubled young man pulling off a bloody T-shirt while the actor playing his father, who Asher recognized as Mr. Howell from *Gilligan's Island*, coddled him. Who did he feel sorrier for, the angsty and misunderstood son or the father who tried too hard while not trying hard enough? He had watched *Rebel without a Cause* ten times previously and still could not decide whether Dean's Jim Stark ever found happiness.

A digital chime chirped at him from his pocket. A text, and one he did not need to look at it to know who sent it. It wearied him to think of a response. He shifted his attention back to the movie, James Dean revving a car's motor in preparation for tearing out to the edge of the cliff. The phone chimed again, guilting him into pulling the device out. *On my way over*, it announced. Sent, as expected, from Jessica, his girlfriend of the last two months. He had known her nearly his entire life, most of it as friends of coincidence, as the margin between friends and enemies felt slim in a high school with less than three hundred students. Three months earlier, feeling self-conscious about going stag to the school's junior-senior prom, he'd asked her to it as his date. Then, almost overnight, she installed herself as his girlfriend, despite no conversation passing between them to signify the upgraded status.

He wanted to text her back and tell her not to come, but that would only speed up her arrival, and darken her increasingly sullen attitude toward him. In the months since the relationship started, she had shifted from friendly conversations to something more controlling, with her personality becoming notably more demanding and tense. He originally planned to bring an end to the pseudo relationship in the days after the prom, but with the introduction of some alcohol to tear down inhibitions, they ended up having sex the night of the event. Then, two days later and back at school, it became common knowledge what they had done, though not from him, and it suddenly felt cruel to end the relationship with that gossip so fresh.

Now, a month later, he continued to fill the role of reluctant boyfriend, with her coming over several mornings a week, always after his mother headed to work. And, unfailingly, once she arrived, they repeated the clumsy coupling that took place on prom night in the back seat of the car he borrowed from his grandmother.

"OK," he texted back, wishing he could watch the rest of the movie without distraction before he needed to shower and head to work.

A sparse ten minutes had passed when the doorknob rattled, followed by a loud and impatient knocking. "Open up," Jessica yelled from the porch while continuing to beat her fist against the door. His mother must have remembered to lock it when she left, or Jessica would have opened it without warning and strutted right in while glaring at the threadbare furniture and shabby walls. Why did she want to date him when she judged his home so openly?

"Hey," Asher offered in a muted greeting as she brushed past him and stepped into the living room.

"Your mom's been smoking in here again," she proclaimed, her nose crinkled in displeasure.

Though it irritated him that his mother smoked in the house, it angered him when someone else commented on it. "It's her house," he replied in a stony tone.

Jessica shrugged her shoulders. "Glad it isn't mine," she countered while rolling her eyes. Then she flashed him a wide, seemingly forced smile. "Come here. You haven't given me a kiss yet," she scolded him. He stepped close and gently slid his arms around her, which she countered by pulling him tight, pushing her mouth hard against his. It always happened this way. She took charge, getting angry if he showed a bit of assertiveness. But despite her aggression, he always noted a melancholy look in her eyes as she did it, as if doubting herself, or compensating for some personal flaw.

She eased up a little, though still maintaining an unyielding embrace. "Do you have to go to your gross job today?" she asked before allowing him to break free.

"In forty-five minutes," he lied, cushioning in an extra hour of freedom from her.

"I thought you worked at noon," she countered, her eyes darkening with mistrust.

"Normally," he sputtered. "They asked me to come an hour early today; breakfast crowds have been bigger than usual."

She shrugged her shoulders, her most common use of body language. "We better hurry," she instructed as she started peeling off her clothes.

Is it like this for everyone? Asher wondered. Neither of them seemed to enjoy it. She acted as if she was forcing out some pent-up aggression while he simply complied. How could a girl who always outwardly seemed polite and gentle prove so demanding and isolated during an act as intimate as this?

As always, it occurred on the ungraciously sagging old sofa, him continuing to watch the movie that played in the background, and her either not noticing or caring. Is this really what everyone was so excited about? Sure, the first time proved arousing, even the first few times after that, but now it felt more akin to a chore, such as doing the dishes or laundry. How did that happen for something that itself felt so good?

"I need to get ready for work," he told her afterward as they sat on the sofa, considerable distance between them. The movie neared its end, and she ignored both him and it, instead texting her friends and, he suspected, sharing with them her just concluded intimacy.

"Fine," she muttered as she stood up, straightening her bra beneath her shirt in the process. He grunted a response, glad to see her go, but also uneasy about her nonchalance. Before they started dating, they frequently chatted about everything going on around them, but the relationship had spurred a callous silence.

"See you later," she offered as she rushed out of the house, not looking back.

He stayed inside the screen door, not following her out onto the porch, watching as she trotted down the steps, then darted across the yard before vanishing down the street. His eyes drifted to the summer foliage that crowded the yard, unkempt bushes clustered against the porch and half a dozen clumps of peak bloom irises in the sunnier corners of the property, ragtag remnants of his great-grandmother's once prized garden.

As a child, he'd toddled through this same yard amazed by its never-ending carnival of color, a splendor spanning March to October. From the initial spring burst of vivid azaleas to the more subtle hues of asters and chrysanthemums in the cooling months, some blossoming beauty could always be found. But in the decade since the gardening matriarch's death, Asher's mother's apathy had all but obliterated the previous beauty. And while he regularly mowed the grass to provide at least a semblance of maintenance on the house's exterior, he felt shame for not doing more to revive a little of the past graciousness.

CHAPTER TWO

"GOOD MORNING, ASHER," a voice offered from the open window of a bright-red Ford pickup truck.

He knew the shiny truck, now conveniently parked along the street he walked every day on his way to work. He also knew the voice.

"Good morning," he gruffly answered without stopping or slowing to engage with his greeter.

"Got a minute?" the man asked. The truck's diesel engine roared to life, and the truck slowly creeped forward in sync with Asher's pace.

Anxious to curtail the interaction, Asher stopped, and the truck did the same. "I've got to go work," he replied in an impatient tone as he peered in through the passenger window, barely making out the shadowy face of the driver.

"I can drive you," the man offered.

"It's less than a block," he countered, exhausted by the unwanted interaction.

The man in the truck nodded. "I heard you work at the diner," he said. "Do you like it?"

Asher shrugged his shoulders, unwilling to share more.

The man in the truck paused in response, so Asher turned away and again started walking.

"Let me know if you ever need anything," the man called out, in what sounded more a cry of desperation than an offer of support.

The gray granite Decatur County Courthouse sat to the left as Asher emerged onto the shabby town square, an antiquated county seat layout with an unkempt park in its core, a public green space populated with a weathered bandstand and a scattering of lichen-marred monuments among poorly pruned foliage. He crossed the street, keeping to the western side of the square, before stopping in the middle of the block of weathered, century-old storefronts, near an edifice painted electric blue and sporting a faded red-and-white-striped aluminum awning. *Time for work.* On most days, the town's venerable greasy spoon proved one of the busiest businesses in the old commercial district, with only the antiquated hardware store that sat opposite the park offering any serious competition.

The red truck drove slowly past as Asher reached the diner's door, so he paused for a moment, watching in the reflection of the door's glass as the vehicle stopped at the end of the street, then turned out of view. He took a calming breath, more in response to being rid of the truck and its driver than in fortifying himself for the next nine hours. Sally, the owner's daughter and the diner's only waitress, shot him a consoling smile as he stepped inside.

"He was in for breakfast and asked what time you come in for work," she told him in a hushed voice as he passed by her on his way to the kitchen. "I didn't know he'd try to ambush you."

It did not bother Asher that everyone in town knew his business, or at least that part of it. He had lived his entire life with the murmuring gossip, so it might feel strange if people stopped talking about it, or if their occasional empathetic looks vanished. Occasionally, one of the do-gooders would try to help his mother and him, with their superiority in full view as they did so, and in turn garnered unabashed resentment from the family of two. Sally's help, or at least willingness to listen, had never been refused. Maybe because she went to school with his mother and still remembered her as pretty, sweet, and caring. Aspects increasingly faded by the last seventeen years of disappointment and failure.

"I put a hamburger and fries on the back table so you can get your belly full before starting your shift," she told him, as if knowing only stale cereal and rancid milk filled the cabinets at home. His first paycheck would arrive the next day, and he would proudly walk to the grocery store on the bypass to stock the kitchen shelves.

"Thank you," he replied, holding back a few tears of gratitude. In a small country town, tears from a boy older than the age of eight gave the appearance of being weak. And he already felt as if he lived a single flaw away from becoming the target of every bully in town. Thus, regardless of the emotion that might build in his chest, any lapse toward public crying must be avoided.

As it was, he had one bully who would not let up—Tommy Summer. But that came from a more personal place than how the common bully picked their prey. Luckily, for those more general offenders, he had two salvations to help shield against unmitigated abuse. First, intelligence, making him the top student in most of his classes and a favorite of teachers and administrators alike. Second, despite the persistent taint of poverty his secondhand clothes and enrollment in his school's free-lunch program presented, the consensus among his peers declared him handsome. The type of handsome that money and a little more awareness for the right haircut and nicer clothes could turn into one of those rare people others unconsciously gaze at.

"The burger has mushrooms and Swiss cheese as you like," Sally offered. She had followed him through the kitchen to the employee break room, a tiny cubby stuffed behind the dishwashing station. "You have the most adult taste of any seventeen-year-old I know."

He smiled at her as he sat at the grimy table where his lunch waited. The fries radiated the warmth of being fresh out of the fryer as Sally knew he always arrived exactly fifteen minutes early.

"I saw your momma last night over at the Wagon Wheel," she remarked. She watched him as he ate, despite the fact a dozen or so customers waited for her out front. "She said you want to go to college. And Mrs. Donovan is helping you find scholarships."

He nodded, a mouthful of the savory hamburger melting in his mouth.

"That's good," she continued. "You need to go to college. Go to college and get a good job." She kept looking at him, then paused a moment. "I hope you're being careful so you don't get stuck in this town," she added.

He looked up at her. "What do you mean?" he asked though he knew she meant Jessica.

"Maybe take it slow with that girlfriend of yours, and if nothing else, use protection," Sally replied. "Your mom's worried."

His face flashed hot with embarrassment. "My mom hasn't said anything to me about it," he responded.

From up front, Sally's father, Sam, yelled for her to get back to work.

"She wouldn't; would she?" Sally countered, giving him a stern look. "You be careful. That girl may be pretty and bubbly, but she's not worth the risk," she added before walking away.

He hurried to finish the burger and fries, but not so hastily as to waste any of it. Not much food waited at home for dinner unless his mom skipped the bar that night and brought something home with her. Or he could call his grandmother, which would get him fed, but also might start a fight between the two women. He carried his plate to the old Hobart dishwasher where he loaded it and a stack from the early lunch crowd for his first cycle of the day.

On the job less than two weeks and still eager to make a good impression. Sally hired him, despite her father's objection—namely an assumption the boy would be flakey like his mother. Of course, his mother never flaked when it involved work. That morning she awoke at nine to be at work by ten, despite probably nursing a hang-over caused by drinks at the Wagon Wheel followed by several of her vodka-heavy screwdrivers once home. She never missed work or showed up late. Half-assed taking care of her kid? Yeah, that happened and routinely letting the pantry run bare at the house, but she drew a line when it might jeopardize her regular paycheck.

The buzz of small talk grew louder from the direction of the dining room. The lunch crush had arrived. Asher grabbed his plastic bin and passed back through the butler's door into a packed restaurant. He shimmied between chairs, grabbing up empty plates and clearing and cleaning any tables as they became vacant. He spotted familiar faces, many of them from the courthouse, the only employer of notable size left on the square, while others had the appearance of the farmers from across the county, in town for court dates or to settle property issues. At a couple of tables in the most out of the way corner sat the daily regulars, mostly old men who drank coffee and gossiped for hours each day, though they would recoil at the use of that word.

"How are you today, Asher?" a friendly voice asked. He turned around to see his English teacher, Mrs. Donovan, sitting at a table with the old man who owned the newspaper.

"I'm well, ma'am," he answered, feeling embarrassed by her seeing him working there, though he did not know why it should.

"I'm glad to see you with a summer job," she continued with an approving smile. "It's a good way to save money for college. I told Mr. Shipley here that this next year you'll be applying for the scholarship his newspaper gives out."

The old man nodded. Asher had seen him many times in his life but had never talked to him. And he knew that on weekends and during the summer months Mrs. Donovan worked part time at his newspaper as a copy editor.

"I'm...I'm very interested in the scholarship," Asher stated, feeling his hands grow sweaty as he held the plastic bin.

"Mrs. Donovan tells me you're a smart young man, and I want to encourage that where I can," the man replied. "Fill out the form when school starts back up in August and have her give it to me."

Asher offered a timid smile, bowed his head, and stepped away to a neighboring table that needed clearing and cleaning.

The newspaper scholarship only provided $350 a semester for the first two years, which seemed a tiny fraction of what it would cost to go to Missouri State University, or Missouri Southern State University over in Joplin, which had a reputation for being considerably less expensive. It would take a lot of $350 scholarships if he ever hoped to get a bachelor's degree. He could start at a junior college, since they cost less, but in two years he would need to transfer to a four-year school, which would mean a jump in cost and would have to happen without the newspaper scholarship. Where could he ever hope to get the money he needed?

Sometimes it felt pointless thinking of college when he did not have enough money to stock the house with generic-brand ramen noodles. But despite the pessimism that often snuck into his thoughts, an optimism also existed, one that drove him to get good grades in school and concoct dozens of daydream futures for himself, all built around a college education.

"Hey, faggot," a voice called to him in a quiet, yet menacing way.

"What, Tommy?" Asher asked, not even glancing around to see who stood behind him.

"Why the hell are they letting white trash near the food?" Tommy inquired, which he followed with a childish giggle. "We're probably going to get the runs from eating here."

Asher stood as tall as he could, as at six feet tall he was not without the ability to intimidate, then turned to face his aggressor. But despite Asher's posturing, the fair-headed Tommy still dwarfed him by several inches, though his smooth moon face gave the appearance of an awed child rather than a menacing goon. Behind Tommy stood three others, all boys in their grade in school, all of whom played football with the antagonist, and two of them wearing goofy grins. Blaine Riley's uneasy frown left him the outlier.

"Leave me alone, Tommy," Asher quietly warned.

The boys, except Blaine, burst into laughter, triggering Sally to quickly make her way to Asher's side.

"What's the problem here?" she asked.

A smirk appeared on Tommy's face. "I'm worried about rats and cockroaches when you have him working here," he spouted, then offered another bellow of laughter.

"Watch yourself," she warned. "I'll tell your father about this behavior."

Tommy snorted. "My dad doesn't tell me what to do, and if he did, he'd be sorry," the boy replied. "Call my mom and tell her you've got this trash working here. She'd tell you what to do with him."

Sally's pale cheeks and forehead flushed a bright red. "Get the hell out of here," she warned them.

"We haven't eaten," Tommy barked back.

"I don't care. All of you, out," she demanded.

The four of them stood still for a moment—Tommy puffed up and self-righteous, the other three edging more toward embarrassed. "Watch it, faggot," he warned Asher as he turned to the door. Blaine paused a moment as the other three left. "I'm sorry," he quietly told him, then followed the others out the door.

Sally sighed and shook her head. "Sorry about that, honey,"

she offered.

"It's okay," Asher answered, his eyes avoiding her from the shame of being so openly demeaned. "I'm used to it."

She slowly shook her head. "That bin is about full; take it back, and check on the dishwasher," she told him, her voice gentle.

Stepping back into the kitchen, he overheard Sam warning his daughter about the "boy" costing him customers.

Tommy Summer first assumed the role of Asher's tormenter in the third grade, the first and only year they shared an elementary school classroom, a placement mistake made by someone unaware of Tommy's mother's engrained bitterness toward Asher and his mother. The second day of that school year, Tommy walked up to him and called him a bastard, following the obscene word with an explanation: "That's what my mom said." Asher had never heard the word before, so he went home and asked his mother. She broke into tears and pulled him into a tight embrace, so tight she made it hard for him to breathe.

Throughout that year, Tommy continued to taunt him and tried to corral other classmates against him, with only limited success. The next year, they returned to separate classes and did not sit together in the same room until junior high, when single classroom learning was replaced with a new teacher and room every period. Mirroring the events of five years earlier, on the first day of their shared seventh grade civics class, Tommy grunted out the insult of "faggot bastard," introducing the new embellishment to his old favorite.

Now, five years later, the hostile behavior continued, as Tommy took every advantage he could to insult and belittle Asher, including regularly calling his mother a whore and drunk. In gym class, he even attempted physical assault. Luckily, despite Tommy having plenty of girth on his side in these altercations, Asher proved faster and more agile, preventing most of the attempts. Only occasionally, usually when Tommy persuaded other boys to help, did he manage notable harm, typically in the form of ripping Asher's clothes, giving him a bloody lip or nose, or on one occasion, cutting off a clump of his hair.

Most of the time, the other boys backed off from Tommy's challenges, an almost ironic behavior for the herd mentality that often led teenage boys to act on or encourage the demeaning of others. Tommy seemed oblivious to this sometimes-tenuous support he had, instead encouraged by his own aggressions.

Asher realized his confidence, intelligence, and good looks had largely protected him from Tommy's insistent onslaught being shared by others. He got along well with most other students at school, shielding his natural introversion by forcing himself to act friendly and talkative. He also proved his worth to the athletes, qualifying for state in track and field in the spring; the academics, with consistent good grades; and with the unpopular outliers, as he tried not to replicate the misery Tommy sought to inflict on him. But, despite his middling popularity, there remained a stigma.

Other students, even those he considered friends, talked behind his back about his poverty, his mother's behavior, and in the quietest whispers, his father.

The late afternoon meant sweeping and mopping the diner's floor, cleaning the appliances, and helping Sally fill bottles, shakers, and napkin dispensers. He enjoyed this part of the workday, as it gave him an opportunity to do mindless work while dreaming of his future, particularly escaping his mother's fate by leaving the town and discovering the rest of the world. In his life, he had never flown on a plane or been farther from home than Kansas City, a mere three-and-a-half-hour drive by car. How could someone understand the world if they'd never seen it?

Sally sat across the table from him, carefully refilling ketchup bottles, aware that Sam would make an ugly remark if he saw mess or waste. Asher had known her his entire life, and unlike most people in town, she never spoke poorly of his mother, despite seeing more of the woman's unpleasant behavior than most.

"Tommy Summer is a little asshole," she remarked without taking her eyes off the slowly filling Heinz Ketchup bottle, though the generic bulk container she used to refill the brand-name bottle called it catsup. "So's his mother. I've known her since the first grade. And I can count on one hand the number of times she's been nice to anyone."

A smile grew across Asher's face. "I don't worry about it," he told her.

Sally nodded.

By 6:00 p.m. the dinner crowd started to arrive, mostly locals out of the house for a meal, though never as many as lunchtime brought, except on Fridays and Saturdays. Asher bounced back and forth between the tables, clearing them off and wiping them down, while growing pangs of hunger soured his mood. He loaded the dishwasher for the sixth time that night, hit start, then pulled his phone out of his pocket. He typed, "When will you be home tonight?" and sent it to his mom. A few seconds passed and an answer came back. She always replied quickly. "Heading to the Wheel; not sure how late," she had responded. He let out a disgruntled sigh. With no food in the house, he would have to find an alternative. He typed, "What are you doing later tonight?" and sent it to Jessica though he winced while doing so. If she came over, he would ask her to stop by the Taco Shop on the bypass and bring him something. She always asked if he wanted her to bring him something to eat. He knew she asked because he was poor, though it seemed one of the few selfless things she still did for him. Before they dated, and, instead, had a friendship, she sometimes bought food for the whole group if he was there, and he always felt she did it specifically for him. But now, when she asked, it felt disparaging.

"Out with Tiff and Jojo" came the reply. "See ya" followed in a second message.

He would not ask his friends, as he vowed to never again ask his friends. They already did plenty to make him seem a charity case. Giving him free sodas and saying the machine gave two or taking him to the movies or a concert under the premise they got free tickets. If it happened occasionally, he would not think anything of it, but it happened almost weekly. He knew someone would feed him tonight if he asked, but he did not want to ask. Not even Sally, because he did not want Sam complaining that he needed to buy the food like everyone else.

He scrolled through his contact list for the right number, and once he found it, dialed.

"Hello," an elderly woman's voice offered in greeting.

"Hi, Grandma," Asher replied.

"Hi, sweetie. How are you?" she asked.

"Fine," he answered, then paused. "Can I come over for dinner?"

CHAPTER THREE

ASHER NOTED THE presence of shimmering tears in Evie Brock's moist eyes as she watched him, her youngest grandson, down forkfuls of her roast beef and potatoes. They sat alone at the kitchen table, as his grandmother, and his Uncle Roland and his wife, Hope, had eaten dinner hours earlier. His grandmother never turned down offering Asher a meal, no matter how late at night. And he suspected she knew that whenever he came asking it meant her only daughter, Bridget, had failed in providing at home.

"Thanks for picking me up, Grandma," Asher said, once he felt sated enough to take a break from eating. He wanted to say more, but he felt guilty for having exposed his mother's most recent failure.

"Of course, honey," she replied, laying her hand on his arm. "All you have to do is ask."

He knew it. She'd offered plenty over the years, including a standing request for him to move out on the farm with her, his uncle, aunt, and cousin. But he could not bear to do that to his mother, who regularly professed that she knew she'd failed him. If he left her to stay with his grandmother, it would openly confirm her failure for both her and everyone who knew them and possibly drive his mother to some tragic extreme.

"Do you think R.J. would give me a ride back into town?" he asked her, referencing his cousin, who, though three years older, still lived at home helping his dad run the farm.

She nodded. "He'd be happy to do it," Evie replied. "He had a date earlier out at the catfish house. A friend of your girlfriend, he said."

Thinking about Jessica exhausted him. He expected sometime around midmorning the next day he'd get a text from her saying she would arrive in ten minutes, after which they would do the only activity she cared to do with him. They had not watched a movie together or gone out, even for a walk around the town square or to a party, in weeks. He'd asked her several times to meet him on his day off or after work, but she always gave an excuse for being busy. Her interactions with him had become increasingly short and controlled, despite remaining frequent.

Evie stood from the table and stepped out of the kitchen. He heard her yelling up the stairs, asking his cousin to give him a ride. The drive of three miles each direction took about fifteen minutes round trip, so he did not feel too guilty in asking for his cousin to take him home, especially as his grandma had already made the trip once that night.

"Hey buddy, you ready?" R.J. asked in a hearty voice as he appeared in the kitchen doorway, their grandmother standing close behind him.

Asher hurried to his feet, not wanting to make his cousin wait, especially after asking him for the favor.

"One minute," Evie warned. "I'll put a plate together that you can take home with you."

R.J. laughed in response to his grandmother's constant need to provide, then stepped over to his cousin and enveloped him in a bear hug. The older cousin had a soft spot for the younger one, consistent in giving him a hug and occasionally passing him a few dollars. Despite dropping out of high school his junior year, R.J. was a hard worker. He never failed to do his share on the farm and kept on the lookout for creative ways to make money on the side, such as selling laying hens to folks in the town. They arrived in little heated chicken coops he built. With an affable nature and friendly face, he typically found some measure of success in his ventures, if sometimes fleeting. But even with R.J.'s open generosity, Asher avoided asking too much in favors, trying to avoid the appearance of a user, or as being unable to take care of himself.

"Still dating Jessica?" R.J. asked once the truck had left the farm behind.

Asher nodded, feeling uncomfortable about the details of his relationship.

"Went out with her friend JoJo earlier," his cousin continued. "She's a hottie, really sweet too. Said she's worried about Jessica."

Jessica's friends all seemed to like him, or at least acted friendly toward him. But they also got quiet when he happened to be around. He felt they shared a secret they did not think he would understand. Sometimes they looked at each other in a way that made him feel they kept it a secret from Jessica too.

"I don't know what that's about," Asher answered. "Jessica doesn't tell me what she talks about with her friends."

R.J., who normally bubbled over with conversation, became quiet for a moment. "JoJo said Jessica has problems at home, really bad stuff," he finally said.

"What do you mean, bad?" Asher asked, surprised by the comment, but realizing it reflected the truth.

"She didn't say much, just it's really bad, and she thinks it's making Jessica act how she does," R.J. replied.

What did that mean, acting how she did? Did it mean her coming over most mornings of the week? Was the problem at home why she hardly texted him or called after five in the evening? Or was he part of the problem? Did he hurt her by being so obliging when she came over, never asking her why she acted the way she did?

"Did you hear what I said?" R.J. asked after a moment of silence between them.

"Yeah," Asher replied. His gut ached with a dull throb. If Jessica's life had something so bad in it, how did he not know? Weren't boyfriends supposed to know their girlfriends? Probably so in healthy relationships, but theirs felt far removed from the ideal. He knew they did not love each other or, increasingly, even like each other. "Is she getting hit, or yelled at, or something else?" he asked his cousin, hoping for a hint or clue.

R.J. grew quiet again, a sign of his discomfort. "I don't know," he muttered. It sounded like a lie, one to protect his younger cousin from some sinister truth.

It did not matter. Asher would not press R.J. any longer. "I probably shouldn't be dating her. I don't think we like each other," Asher offered this truth, a relief to tell someone rather than keeping it to himself.

"Been there," R.J. replied with a slight laugh. "I dated a couple girls just because I was bored, but those never lasted more than a few weeks." He pulled the truck to a stop in front of Asher's house.

"Remember how pretty this house was when Nana lived here?" Asher asked. "Flowers everywhere and her bright-orange lawn chairs."

The two-bedroom cottage once had the appearance of a gardener's showplace, even when a faded old mobile home, where

Asher and his mother had lived for seven years, sat in the yard beside it. When their great-grandmother died, the family, largely out of pity, gave the house to his mother. Now, ten years later, all the beauty had faded away, leaving the property downright derelict.

"I do," R.J. answered.

Shame rose from Asher's heart and settled in the back of his throat, tightening it to almost choking. Shame for the fact he did so little to take care of the property, other than a minimum of mowing the lawn and occasionally picking up random trash that blew into it. "Can you bring the lawnmower over on Friday?" he asked

R.J. nodded, embarrassment reddening his face. "It looks okay, now," he said.

"No, it doesn't," Asher protested. "It looks abandoned." He climbed out of the truck and crossed the dew-covered grass, his legs heavy as he did so. He felt as if some force tried to hold him back from the gray hovel that sat dingy and sagging on a street dimmed by the lack of working streetlamps.

The boards of the porch creaked as he crossed, and the doorknob turned easily. Unlocked. Three or four hours earlier, his mother, perhaps absent-mindedly, must have forgotten to lock it on her way out for a night at the bar. Though they had little to steal, he always made a point of locking the door when he left, a hopeful habit for a more prosperous future. A behavior his mother, at least subconsciously, deemed pointless.

He felt around the corner for the light switch, clicking it on and bringing into view the uncomfortably warm living room. The house had no air-conditioning, not even a window unit, so in the deepest days of summer it could feel warmer inside than outside. He leaned over and turned on the old box fan, a holdover from his great-grandmother. Someday soon, he expected it to burn out, but for now it worked, rattling and squealing as the blades turned, while pushing out almost enough breeze that one could be nearly comfortable sitting on the couch.

Reaching the kitchen, he turned on the light above the sink, revealing a plastic bag sitting on the countertop. He opened the bag and peeked inside, finding three carefully wrapped tacos. She had not forgotten his dinner. Here it sat, waiting for him. Tears bubbled up in his eyes and a sob escaped him. He'd needlessly embarrassed her to her own mother. He'd expected the worst, without checking to see if she brought something for him. The tears trickled down his face. A ridiculous reaction, he knew, as plenty of times in the past those tacos had not been there, forcing him to either reach out to others for food or go hungry. Why did he feel so overwhelmed now? It made no sense. He deserved better, didn't he? He deserved to never need to worry about there being food at home, especially if she only planned to spend her money on drinks at the bar or on cigarettes. Three tacos didn't make up for those countless occasions, yet he sniffled as if he were a child with a skinned knee.

He took a step away from the counter and let his eyes dry, but the tacos stared at him. He could not leave them uneaten. She'd bought them for him. But he also had a full belly and plate of left-overs from his grandmother. If his mom saw those in the refrigerator, she would know he had dinner there. He had no appetite, but still picked up a taco and ate it. Fast food and salty, but easy to eat. He had a second, noting his gut now neared capacity. Then he picked up the third one and took a couple bites. He forced himself to take a third bite. He had eaten half of it; any more would make him puke. He shoved the remaining half into the plastic bag and tossed it into the trash.

The plate from his grandmother remained. It could be lunch tomorrow, or possibly dinner, if his mother went to the bar again, and left nothing for him to eat, as often happened. He could put it into the refrigerator, but in that empty box she would spot it instantly, with nowhere to hide it except behind her orange juice and vodka. Or he could take it to his room, but in the hot house it would spoil by the time he wanted it. The only reasonable answer pained him. He carried the plate to the trash and scraped its contents into the bin, then put crumpled-up newspaper on top of the discarded meal to conceal it.

His chest felt hollow thinking of the food he'd wasted and how his actions earlier that night added to his grandmother's disgust with her daughter. Sweat darkened his T-shirt, from both the swampy atmosphere of the house and the embarrassment he felt toward himself. He went to his bedroom and closed the door, then peeled the shirt off. He paused for a moment, gazing at himself in the mirror. The beauty others complimented him on seemed elusive. His dark, thick hair hung damp and greasy over his forehead, his deep brown eyes looked glossy and sunken behind puffy red flesh, his mouth held a sour downturned shape with a wisp of facial hair dirtying his upper lip and chin, and his sweaty skin dared pimples to pop up. He took a deep breath, watching his chest rise and then fall. Even his body taunted him, tired and exhausted, despite the daily regimen of push-ups, sit-ups, and running he underwent for the last three months of the school year.

Did he really believe he would ever leave this town? He belonged here, bussing tables and living in a shabby house, sharing his mother's aimlessness. Why should he expect more? Those who told him otherwise only humored him, whether intentionally or subconsciously, doing their minimum to bring him to a miserable maturity. Look at the meth heads that populated the county—had they not been the same as him once, too, expecting a bright future, but seeing it shattered when reality hit? Who could he name that made it out? Meade Donovan, his English teacher's son, left but only after getting beaten up at school for being gay. His leaving did not mean he would accomplish anything—maybe he just moved his misery someplace marginally better where he wasn't the favorite target for a small town's homophobes.

Asher switched off the light and lay down on his bed. The thought of the tacos came to him again, and tears flooded his eyes. *What a wimp*, he told himself in an effort to shame his emotions away. He turned over onto his side, trying to shift his mind to better thoughts. His old standby emerged in his imagination, the idea of owning his own business. Maybe a bed and breakfast somewhere, a place with history, and a front porch with a view of nature. Unrealistic, yes, but maybe a place to work toward. And if that one scenario should prove a fantasy, there were hundreds of other ways he might find contentment.

His phone chimed from another room. He must have left it on the kitchen countertop. With an exhausted sigh, he got back on his feet and staggered out of his bedroom, quickly spotting the phone sitting by the sink.

Tommy's a real jerk, the message read. It came from Blaine.

It's fine, used to it, Asher responded.

You alright? Blaine asked.

Yeah, Asher typed back, then dropped his phone into his pocket.

He stepped into the living room and turned off the fan, not in the mood to watch television tonight.

He and Blaine had been off-and-on best friends since the second grade, though more often off in the last few years, as the spoils of puberty had sent Blaine in the direction of whichever pretty girl was closest. With that change, Asher found they had less to talk about, even as he increasingly wanted to spend time with his newly athletic friend. In that, Asher knew he felt differently from most of the boys at his school, as while he struggled to hide his glances at their shirtless torsos in the locker room, they gushed about the blossomed maturity of the girls they knew.

CHAPTER FOUR

JESSICA'S EYES BLINKED slowly and apathetically, and her pale face was absent of anger's red flush, despite the rise in volume of her voice as she declared Asher white trash and pointedly criticized his indigent appearance. Her reaction to him ending their relationship sounded almost rehearsed, as if she'd decided weeks earlier exactly what to say when the time came. For behind the tough words, an emotion more akin to relief emerged through her relaxed posture and calm expression.

He told her he missed being her friend and believed neither really wanted the relationship. She did not interrupt, instead sinking comfortably onto his sofa as he elaborated on his reasoning far more than needed. Once he finished, she briefly returned to her faux-offended script, including uttering a low-grade slur, as if to show she still held some control in the relationship. Then, the necessities out of the way, a smile crept onto her face and she stood. The smile suggested an apology. She then walked across the room to the front door, from which she glanced back at him before stepping out onto the porch.

For several seconds, he did not move, allowing her time to escape; then he stepped up to the open door and watched as she crossed the yard to the street. His decision to end the relationship came to him that morning as he thought back on the conversation with his cousin the previous night. If he really felt the way he said he did, to continue dating her not only felt disingenuous but would hurt them both in the future.

No more girlfriend, and no more detached, unemotional sex. He paced back to the sofa and collapsed down onto it in a lazy slump, grabbing up the television remote once he found a point of exhausted comfort. His mom never missed paying the satellite bill. Probably for the same reason she always had enough money to buy vodka and cigarettes—her escapes from reality. A reality of which he made up the largest part. Nothing on the television interested him, so he stood and stretched, noticing the clock showed 10:00 a.m. He did not work until noon, but his first paycheck already waited for him at the diner.

"Homeless," the word Jessica used to describe how he dressed and looked. It cut more than the vulgar comments she'd made, as he knew his appearance, same as the unkempt yard, was avoidable. But he had done little to rectify it, as he typically wore his clothing beyond threadbare, seldom added gel to his hair, and currently sported a scraggly and thin assortment of freshly sprouted facial hair, a development so new he had never before picked up a razor. Three or four months prior, that last concern had not been a noticeable problem. But a maturing body changed that as his peach fuzz progressed past downy softness to an increasing coarseness, which, at a distance, made his face look dirty.

After a quick shower and procuring the loan of a bicycle from the neighbor across the street, he peddled in the direction of the diner to collect his paycheck. He had earned money before, helping his cousin R.J. mow lawns and working on the farm for his uncle, but never as an official employee, earning a taxable income every two weeks. And despite his lowly role of dishwasher and busboy, the thought of having a job made him feel nearly an adult. It meant he achieved at least some self-sufficiency. A check, with his name on it, waited for him, though he already knew it wouldn't break $350 for two weeks work.

"Hi, honey, what're you doing here so early?" Sally asked as he walked into the restaurant.

He bit down on his bottom lip to keep from smiling at the thought of receiving his first check. "It's payday," he muttered, feeling his face warm with embarrassment.

She smiled. "It is. Wait here, and I'll grab your check," she told him before disappearing into the kitchen. Half a dozen customers sat spread out at a few tables and the counter, the late breakfast crowd. Everyone had turned their head to see who entered when he arrived. He never worked breakfast, as Sam said they had plenty of dishes to get them through without paying some kid who could just as easily wash them later.

"Here you go," Sally announced as she returned with two envelopes in her hand. He took them from her. One felt thin and had a clear window on the front, through which he saw his name printed, and the second weighed notably heavier in his hand. "What's this?" he asked as he held the heftier envelope up to her.

"Have a look," she answered with a broad smile.

He opened the envelope and inside found fifty dollars in cash: two tens, two fives and what he would later count as twenty ones. "I don't understand," he replied.

"Your share of the tips," she told him in a quiet voice, then winked at him. He wanted to hug her, instead settling for returning the smile. He knew this came from her, because Sam sternly told him when he started that dishwashers did not get tips.

"Thank you," he offered, feeling his eyes grow misty. She patted him on the shoulder and nodded to the door. He then obediently followed her direction before Sam could become suspicious.

Back on the bike, with giddiness overtaking him, Asher took off at full speed. The bank, the only place he could think of to cash his check, was two miles away on the bypass. Years earlier, before he started elementary school, the bank operated out of a building on the town square. A big chunk of a place with massive windows that extended up two stories and a bronze frieze of a farmer inlaid above the double doors that led into the lobby. He remembered going inside the old bank with his grandmother a few times and always feeling awed by the cavernous space.

He confidently zoomed out of the decaying town core, across the railroad tracks and by the fast food restaurants, strip malls, and new high school. He veered to the right and into the parking lot of the current bank building, which had abandoned the gravitas of the old, minimized to a one-story tan brick edifice with a drive-through window. No more heavy gold drapes or marble floors to impress its clients, just carpet, tile, and laminate surface. He nervously glanced around the lobby, uncertain of what to do next.

"Hi, Ash," a friendly voice greeted him. A girl from school sat behind one of the teller windows, waving at him in an almost frantic manner. He gave her a timid wave back and started toward her, but another customer stepped up to her window before he could get there. In the window to her right sat a woman in her late thirties. She had no customer and gave him an icy stare, taunting him to make up his mind on what to do and not willing to offer any help in getting him there. He swallowed hard and stepped up to face her.

"How can I help you?" she asked, her frosty blue eyes evaluating his ragged appearance.

"I need to cash my paycheck," he told her, trying to project confidence by meeting her gaze.

"Account number?" she asked him.

His body went rigid; he had neither an account number nor account. "I don't have one," he mumbled.

"An account number or an account?" she questioned, her face stiffening to extenuate her annoyance.

"Neither," he answered. The sweat from his bike ride, which had nearly vanished thanks to the bank's robust air-conditioning, re-erupted across his body.

"We only cash checks for customers with accounts," she informed him. "Would you like to open an account?"

A bank account, another step toward adulthood. "What do I need for that?" he asked.

"As little as twenty-five dollars and a state or federal identification," she explained.

He had that. "Then I can cash my check and get my money?" he asked.

She tilted her head, as if explaining something ridiculously basic to a child. "With a new account, we have to make sure the check clears first, unless it's a check from this bank," she told him.

Asher tore the envelope open, and there in the bottom corner, he spotted the same bank's logo and address. "It is," he replied with a smile. He took the check from the envelope and laid it on the counter in front of her, feeling proud of his success. "And it doesn't cost me anything to have an account?"

The woman's nose wrinkled as her eyes rolled up in a condescending look. "Keep a minimum balance of $5,000 in it, and it won't cost you anything, otherwise it's ten dollars a month," she answered.

He shook his head and sighed. For most people, ten dollars may not be a lot, but for him, it equaled a couple meals. "Is there someplace I can cash it where I don't need an account?" he asked.

An audible *humph* came from the woman as her eyes narrowed in response to her growing annoyance. "There's a place in the grocery store," she offered. "But they'll charge 10 percent of the check."

It's my money, he thought as he stepped back from the teller's window. Why should cashing a paycheck seem so daunting? He shuffled across the lobby, thinking about what to do, but also trying to avoid the teller's glaring eyes. Was there not a less costly way to collect your own wages?

"What's wrong, Ash?" the girl from school asked him. She smiled at him from behind her window, her customer now gone.

"I'm trying to get my paycheck cashed, but I can't because I don't have an account," he told her as he walked up to her window.

Her eyebrows lifted in surprise. Her name was Lela, he remembered.

"You have an account," she matter-of-factly replied.

She must be thinking about someone else. "No. I've never had one," he explained as he shook his head.

Now, irritation showed as she cocked her head slightly to one side, as if stunned by some new level of stupidity. "You're Asher Alvin Brock, aren't you?" she asked.

He nodded. She then asked him for his birthdate and the last four digits of his social security number. All matched.

"There's been an account here in your name for ten years, set up in March of 2000," she explained.

His grandmother must have set it up for him or, though less likely, his mother, and then never told him about it.

"I can cash my check?" he asked, relieved by the discovery.

"Sign the back," she answered, a big smile on her face. "Do you want to know the current balance of your account?"

How could there be a balance? His mom had no money, and he never knew it existed. "There's money in it?" he questioned her.

Lela nodded. "Do you want to know how much?" she asked again.

"I guess," he replied, his voice little more than a whisper.

She pulled out a piece of paper, wrote something on it, then slid it over to him.

He read "$31,465." *This is not true*, he thought. *How could I have that much money in a bank account?* "Where did it come from?" he asked.

The astonished look reappeared. "Tom Summer puts $250 into it every month," she told him. "That's how I knew you had an account here. He's also the one who set it up for you."

Asher's face hardened, and his hands began to shake. "Why the hell is he doing that?" he growled.

"He's your dad, isn't he?" she said, not as a question, but a statement.

The room grew hot, despite the chill of the air-conditioning. "Can I please just cash my check?" he asked, his voice terse, though he realized Lela did not deserve his now coarse attitude.

"Here you go," she offered a moment later, sliding the pile of cash across the countertop to him. "Do you want to take out anything additional from your account?" Her wary smile a sign that she now understood the awkwardness of the situation.

"I don't want any of that money," he replied.

CHAPTER FIVE

PROFANITIES FLOWED FROM Asher's mouth as he hastily peddled the bicycle back home. In his anger, he forgot to go to the supermarket to pick up food for the weekend, the main reason he borrowed the bike in the first place. That concern had vanished upon his discovery that for the last decade Tom Summer had secretly squirreled money away for him, or at least in his name.

A coward of a man who never once publicly claimed paternity, yet secretly set aside a hoard of money in his illegitimate child's name. What did it mean? Asher knew about the checks to his mother, and that she cashed them every month, but not without enough shame that she would deny having done so. How would queen bee Amanda Summer feel if she knew her husband had banked aside thirty grand for his bastard child? She would probably erupt in one of her infamous angry and ugly scenes, while calling on her own son to up the bullying on his brother and then return to her hobby of making nasty phone calls to his mother in the middle of the night. Though that prank might be tougher now, as his mom only used a cell phone, the landline having been disconnected years earlier due to nonpayment.

A car honked at him, startling him from his distraction and reminding him to steer the bike away from the center of the road. He could see his house, half a block away. A gray truck, his cousin's, sat in the driveway, and the jovial young man himself sat on the porch in a rickety wicker chair, one that had belonged to their great-grandmother.

Asher rode the bike across the lawn and came to a stop at the foot of the porch steps. "What are you doing here?" he asked, his voice distant and preoccupied.

"Hey, cuz," R.J. called out to him as he pointed at their grandmother's lawnmower sitting in the back of his truck.

"Oh, right," Asher replied.

His cousin nodded. "I'm supposed to ask you to come to dinner tonight," he added. "Granny is making it late so you can be there, and Raina is coming too."

Raina, R.J.'s older sister, lived in Springfield and worked as an emergency room nurse, having finished college six months earlier. She always doted on Asher, while conversely teasing her brother, yet they all got along well.

"I don't have a way out there," Asher replied.

"Raina's coming by the diner at nine thirty to get you," R.J. answered.

A plan for everything, with Asher the last to know it. "Why are we having dinner together?" he asked.

R.J. shrugged his shoulders. "Granny wants to," he answered.

Their grandmother never made plans without a reason, so either R.J. did not know the real intent, or he wanted to avoid talking about it. And, with his sometimes obtuse nature, it could be either.

Asher returned the neighbor's bicycle while his cousin rolled the lawnmower to the sagging garden shed in the backyard. An ancient building cluttered with rusty old lawn tools and dusty boxes of canning jars, twenty years out of use. When the wind blew hard, the old shed would rattle, signaling an approaching and inevitable collapse.

An hour later, after climbing out of R.J.'s truck, Asher paused for a moment to note the cars parked in front of the diner, finding comfort in not seeing those of either Tom or Tommy Summer. If he ran into either one of them while in his present mood, he would have a hard time restraining himself from publicly revealing the secret bank account. A circumstance that would prove embarrassing for the father and could lead to destructive repercussions if told to the son.

A hearty contingent of customers filled nearly three quarters of the restaurant's tables, a profitable Friday lunch crowd. The type of day that pleased even cranky old Sam. In fact, a smile was almost detectable on the man's wrinkled face, as he lorded over the cash register.

"Hiya, hon," Sally greeted Asher, as she weaved between tables while holding a tray of plates. "I got a plate of lunch for you in the back. Eat first, then get started on the dishes."

He nodded and made his way across the room, suddenly feeling self-conscious of what Lela said at the bank. If she knew his parentage, then everybody knew. Did they look at him now and think, "There's Tom Summer's bastard"? Some did, he knew, especially those close to Amanda Summer, who had waged battle against him since before his own birth. The woman had thrived on eighteen years of demeaning and degrading a child, using her own son as a proxy for her wrath. Those who disagreed with her hardline method, of which there were a fair amount, typically felt pity for him more than anything else. A fatherless boy, at least in practice, with a mother who drank too much and barely kept herself together. If he asked them what they saw in his future, they might assume drugs, alcohol like his mother, a pregnant girl, jail, or another similar dreary prospect. He had never smoked pot, and had no plans to, and while he had snuck a drink or two with friends, his mother gave him a disheartening example of overindulgence in that.

The burger tasted bland as his mind continued to churn with

thoughts of the discovery of the bank account, and the reminder of the widespread awareness of his own genetics. It was fair for him to be ignorant of the bank account, but embarrassingly naïve of him to assume his father's identity remained a mystery for those who knew him, including his classmates. Most people in the town would have known long before he did. In the second grade, after a third day in a row of being bullied by Tommy Summer, he went to his grandmother in tears, and she told him the secret his mother never had, still had not, at least formally. He'd asked his mom one time, after seeing her take a check from Tom Summer, why he gave her money. She only replied, "Because he owes me." Child support, hush money, or something else to ease the man's conscience, probably the same reason for the $30,000 in the bank. A weak man's attempt to buy away his responsibilities. His wife would probably divorce him if she knew about the account and how much it contained.

Asher picked up his empty lunch plate and carried it to the dishwasher, setting it on the growing pile of soiled dinnerware. Then he pulled on an apron to get to work. Washing dishes held no grandeur or prestige, but he felt a sense of accomplishment in doing it, even if old Sam constantly kept a critical eye on him. Sam liked to judge, as he continued to maintain a nearly eighteen-year grudge against Asher's mother, quietly muttering promiscuous-based insults when he caught a glimpse of her, despite having his own known flaws constantly swirling around him. For instance, he had developed into a skilled creeper, leering at the young women coming into his restaurant, and purposely perching high up behind his register to steal glimpses down loose-fitting blouses. But in his aged mind, Bridget Brock's poor choice in a boyfriend as a seventeen-year-old girl sustained as an unforgivable sin, while he ignored his own perversions. Fortunately, Sally helped temper her father's uncouth behavior, for despite knowing his mother's failings, she never uttered disparagements.

"Get out and bus tables; Sally can't do it all," came Sam's abrupt growl. The man had left his vigil at the register to come back and offer the cranky comment. Asher nodded and grabbed a bin, then hustled past his boss, who watched with the glare of a scowling gargoyle.

"He went back there just to yell at you, didn't he?" Sally quietly asked as she bent over a newly vacated table, helping Asher clear it.

He shrugged in response.

"Don't worry. I'll handle that tonight," she continued. She took a step back and watched as he swabbed the crumbs and mess off the tabletop with his bleach-soaked rag.

"It's all right," he offered, as Sam's actions honestly felt minor compared to his other concerns.

"No, it's not," she countered. "I'll talk with him. And if he treats you that way again after tonight, you tell me."

The sternness in her voice told him she took the matter seriously. But what would she do to make it stick, threaten to walk out?

Threaten to expose some dirty little secret of her own father? Again, it all felt minor. Maybe someday a boss acting like that toward him would feel offensive, but right now it felt the norm and in agreement with how much of the town seemed to view him.

An hour and a half later, after the lunch rush ebbed to one full table and a regular slowly gnawing away at his food while seated at the lunch counter, Asher sat down at a table across from Sally to help roll napkins and refill condiment bottles.

"My grandma is having me come to a late dinner at her house tonight, with my aunt, uncle, and two cousins," he said. "Something's going on."

Sally shook her head, an act of frustration, not disagreement. "Has there been trouble between your mom and grandma recently?" she asked.

Asher sighed. "Yes, but it wasn't Mom's fault," he replied. Sally placed her hand on top of his. He thought about the tacos, how he'd called his grandmother without checking to see if there would be food at home first. It must be related. "Did you know Tom Summer has put money in a bank account with my name on it for ten years?"

Her eyes widened, and she let out a quiet laugh. "I bet Amanda would explode if she knew that," she responded. "How much?"

Maybe he should not have mentioned it. "Enough to pay for four years at Missouri State," he admitted, surprising himself that he equated the money with the cost of a college education. A subconscious revelation. "I'm not going to use it. I don't want his money."

Sally leaned back in her chair, taking a pause from filling bottles. "Why not?" she questioned.

His face grew warm with anger, not at her, but at the situation. "I don't want his guilt money," he growled.

She nodded in understanding, if not agreement.

CHAPTER SIX

THE EXTRA TWO hours of waiting to eat dinner left Asher's family especially famished, with everyone aggressively digging into his grandmother's cooking as if it had been weeks since they last ate. Everyone except Asher, at least. While he felt hungry and ate along with them, his unease restrained his appreciation for the meal, and his gaze jumped from person to person, as he tried to figure out the reason for them all being there.

"Did you enjoy it?" his grandmother asked as she picked up his only partially finished plate.

He nodded.

"I'm glad. I've got some chocolate pie for dessert," she continued.

"That sounds good," he replied with a smile.

His grandmother and aunt cleared the table, leaving the other four to sit quietly, barely speaking a word as they waited for the two older women to sit back down. Every face appeared dour, save R.J.'s, who looked embarrassed and out of place.

"We have something we want to ask you," his grandmother finally said to break the silence once she and his aunt had come back to the table.

Something to ask, Asher thought. *Something to ask without his mother in the room; she's likely not aware the entire family had dinner without her.*

"Okay," he replied.

"We know it's not easy for your mom," his uncle Roland began. "She tries; we know she does, but you deserve more stability than she's able to offer you."

This again? Not the first time a similar discussion had taken place, or second, or third. He didn't answer or move his head to suggest agreement, disagreement, or any other encouragement to continue.

"Raina's living in Springfield now, so her bedroom here at the farm is available," Roland continued.

Asher turned to Raina, whose firm look melted as their eyes met, leaving him to blink away his tears. That was why she came down, to give some sort of blessing for him to have her room. In the past, when this same suggestion came about, he would have had to share a room with R.J., or sleep on the couch. But, with Raina out on her own, an easy answer existed—he could take her room.

"What about my mom?" he asked, his voice trembling as he spoke.

His grandmother sighed. "She'll still have her house, and you can see her any time you want," she explained.

"She would hate it," he countered.

"It's not about her," Roland insisted. "This is about you—this is about you having food to eat, and someone keeping an eye on you. We know you don't need to be told to study, or when to go to bed; you're smart and motivated, but you need more security than she's able to give you."

He felt as if a concrete block dropped onto his stomach. He could not breathe. He could not stand up. He sat startled—startled by the truth in what his uncle said. Not a single word false—all true— all what often ran through his own thoughts. Thoughts he would never share with his mother. She struggled too much already. A life full of disappointments. An adulthood founded on the fact that a high school boy got two girls pregnant at the same time, then married the other one. He married the other because her father offered him a job and a house. How could Asher, Bridget Brock's only child, be expected to leave her, at least now, with only a year of high school left? She was abandoned once before—left with him and a future with no security.

"I won't leave her alone," Asher pushed back.

His grandmother shook her head. "I know you love her, but love yourself too," she told him.

With a loud *whap*, he slammed his hand down on the top of the table. "I won't abandon her, not now," he argued back. "Yes, if I go to college, I'll have to leave, but not before. She already feels like a failure. If I leave her to come here, it'll only make her feel more so. I leave her to go to college, maybe she'll feel she's been successful."

More arguing and urging from his family bubbled up in response. But both they and he knew his decision, as the looks on their faces showed they no longer held hope for persuading him, despite it being the best option for him.

Tears flooded his grandmother's eyes as she looked at him from across the table. This woman, who wore a stoic demeanor as if born with it, and he could never remember having seen her cry, yet now she did. Did his refusal hurt her that much?

"You're a good son," she finally said, her voice rough with emotion. He now realized she did not cry because he said no to her, but because he could not leave his mother. Even though his grandmother knew he would be better off at the farm, his loyalty and concern for her daughter had ignited her emotions more. "If you're staying there, I'm bringing over groceries at least once a week," she told him. "I don't care what your mother says about it."

Asher shook his head. "I have money now from my job. I can buy them," he protested.

"Save that for college," she replied. "I'm buying groceries. And, closer to the start of school, we'll get you some new clothes. You've turned into such a handsome young man, but with your fuzzy face, messy hair and shabby clothes, you look homeless."

He smiled and let out a laugh. He did need to start taking better care of himself. He didn't want to appear...well...white trash. "I wanna go to the thrift store Raina goes to, the one with nice clothes but Walmart prices," he suggested with a smile. His cousin winked at him in response.

"I can get you a whole new wardrobe there for, like, seventy-five dollars," Raina announced. "Good stuff, too, from all the snooty mall shops with tags still on and everything."

The weight on his stomach eased. He sensed renewed support from his family sitting around the table. Even R.J., who had remained largely quiet throughout the discussion, nodded his head with pride for his younger cousin's strength.

Raina volunteered to take him home on her way back to Springfield, and the entire time she gave him instructions on dressing better, which only came across as slightly condescending. As they neared his house, they both grew quiet, surprised to see that his mother had either not gone to the bar or come home early from it, with the porch and living room lights blazing and casting a glare across the front lawn. Raina pulled into the driveway behind his mom's battered 1998 Plymouth Neon. "Should I come inside and say hi?" his cousin asked.

Asher shook his head. "She's probably drunk and would try to talk you into having a drink and staying the night," he warned.

Raina frowned, obviously not interested in spending the night with her alcoholic aunt, who would relentlessly badger her about guys she was dating or her hair and fashion preferences. It had happened several times before, and always made Raina uncomfortable.

He opened the car door and stepped out onto the gravel driveway, holding a heaping plate of food his grandmother had sent along with him. He waited until his cousin drove away before he climbed the steps up onto the porch. A conversation between two distinct voices could be heard inside the house. She had some man in there. Asher took a deep breath and stomped across the porch, pausing to glare through the screen door into the living room.

"That you, Ash?" his mother asked from inside.

"Yeah," he answered.

"It's a Friday night, so I figured you were out with your friends," she continued.

He could count on one hand the number of Friday nights in the last year when he stayed out late with friends.

The screen door opened with a screech, its hinges long in need of oiling, and he stepped into the living room. A rough-looking man clad in dingy jeans and a faded Bud Light T-shirt, one featuring a bull terrier mascot the company discontinued decades earlier, sat on the sofa next to his mom. "What's happening, champ?" the man slurred under a heavy, untrimmed mustache, with the rest of his face a good four or five days from its last shave.

"I had dinner at Grandma's," Asher told his mom but ignored the man on the sofa beside her. He looked down at the plate in his hand. His grandmother had sent it for him to have tomorrow, but it felt rude to keep it for himself. "She sent this for you," he offered as he held out the plate to his mother.

Bridget stood and took it from him with a smile, though a forced one.

She retained a slight figure, despite doing little to keep in shape, but her face seemed increasingly worn, especially in the last few years, as the frequency of her visits to the bar after work increased.

The more independent he became, such as the more time he spent working on homework or involved in track, the more she drifted away. During his elementary school years, she had dinner ready for him every night. She attended his events at school and took him places like Silver Dollar City in Branson a couple times each summer. But his adolescence and her extended loneliness coincided in an unhealthy way. Lots of nights at the bar and a growing roster of men and half-assed dates. Most proved more interested in getting her in bed than in a relationship, which could flip her outgoing, flirty personality to something more akin to cold and combative. In fact, he could count on one hand the number of her relationships that he assumed made it to the consummation stage. Thus, this man must be new to town, or he would have stayed away based on the bitter reviews of the dive bar's regulars.

"She sent this for me?" his mother asked, doubt on her face.

Asher nodded, afraid she would sense the lie if he spoke.

"Bring me a couple of forks, and I'll share it with Randy here," she said as she set the plate on the coffee table. "Unless you want some too?"

Asher shook his head and stepped into the kitchen to get a couple forks out of the flatware drawer. Randy, he thought to himself, probably randy in more than one regard. Back in the living room, Randy leaned back into the couch as he lit up one of Bridget's menthols.

"Wait, babe," Bridget cautioned. "Ash doesn't want anyone to smoke in the house when he's here."

Randy took a long drag off the cigarette and then blew out a stream of smoke. "Ash's a goddamn kid; he doesn't make the rules," he argued.

No civility with this one, Asher thought. "I'm going to my room, Mom," he told her as he handed her the forks, though his eyes burned into the disrespectful visitor. No point in causing more unrest than necessary.

"Smart kid," Randy called out in a mocking tone, followed by a laugh.

"He lives here too, so he has a say," Bridget demanded.

Anger flared in Randy's eyes. "No little shit decides where I smoke," he growled.

Bridget stood, looking down at the surly man splayed out on the sofa. "It's time you left," she insisted.

Randy angrily bolted up, and with a hard shove sent Bridget tumbling back down onto the sofa. "How dare you, you little bitch!" he yelled.

The attack sent a surge of anger through Asher's body. He needed a weapon to protect her, and the carving knife came to mind. He ran to the kitchen and yanked on the handle of a cabinet drawer, launching it halfway across the room and crashing onto the floor, scattering utensils everywhere. He had not meant to use that much force. The big knife lay in front of the refrigerator, so he lunged for it. Possibly aware of Asher's intentions, Randy rushed at him. The older man kicked hard against Asher's side, sending him flying across the room and crashing into the back door, which emitted a loud cracking in response. The drunk man then strode over to him and towered over his crumpled body where he lay on the floor. "Time to teach you a lesson, boy," he threatened. Randy began to lean over, his massive hand grasping at Asher, but then stopped and let out a pained scream.

A few feet behind the big man, Bridget stood trembling with the knife in her hand, a few drops of blood trickling off its sharp tip. "You touch him, and I'll stick it in deep," she warned. Randy swung toward her and made a quick lunge in her direction, but she acted faster and slashed the knife against his open palm, causing him to jump back with a pained yelp. "Get out," she warned him again.

His stunned and drunken frame swayed back and forth a moment, as if deciding what move to make next. The risk must have seemed too great, so he turned and stomped out of the kitchen and across the living room, but not without kicking the coffee table over, knocking the food to the floor and shattering the plate.

"Nothing but a bar tramp," Randy yelled back as he kicked the screen door open before disappearing into the dark night.

The knife slipped from Bridget's hand and dropped to the floor, giving her the freedom to help Asher back onto his feet. "I'm so sorry, honey. I had no idea he'd act that way," she said between sobs, her arms tightly holding onto him.

She never thought they would act the way they did. Each drunk she met and brought home for a nightcap always started off as a Prince Charming in her lonely mind. Someday, she insisted, she would find the one, the one who could make her happy. And while Randy proved a bit more violent than most, the trajectory of the night's events had past precedent in the house. But despite a need for better vetting in who she invited over, Asher credited her for quickly ejecting the most obvious mistakes. The violent ones, the erratic ones, the one who followed him into the bathroom when he was thirteen and tried to grope him as he peed. That last one left with a likely concussion, caused by a frying pan against the head, the first time she showed her willingness to use a weapon when necessary. Despite this history of failure, she continued to hold out hope that someday one of the barflies would amount to something.

Asher felt a sore tinge in his side where he was kicked and in his shoulder where he hit the door, but nothing felt too serious, just bruised, so he put his arm around his mom's shoulders and walked her back into the living room.

"Sorry about the food," he told her, looking down at his grandmother's broken plate and the mess on the floor.

Bridget shook her head. "No big deal, but Mama will flip about the plate," she replied. She led him to the sofa and told him to sit, after which she cleaned up the mess. With the broken dish and spoiled food in the trash, she sat back beside him and turned on the television. Then, for the next few hours, in almost complete silence, they watched a series of old sitcom reruns, favorites from her childhood, and she did not smoke a single cigarette or drink a drop of alcohol the entire time.

CHAPTER SEVEN

A MONTH FULL of days at work and lazy hours on the sofa passed in the wake of his breakup with Jessica. That change in his relationship status had generally been a relief, though, at times, he did miss the physical side of it. Of course, as a healthy seventeen-year-old, he proved well skilled at taking care of that problem himself, though he now understood why his mother often missed the touch of another.

On a sunny, hot Saturday morning, he had yet to climb out of bed, so with a sigh of some regret, he rolled his legs off the edge and sat up. His alarm clock showed as nearly ten a.m., so work started in two hours, or an hour and forty-five minutes if he wanted to eat lunch at the diner first. Old Sam had eased off him in recent weeks, a change he attributed to Sally, who must have given her father an ultimatum as she no longer hid that he got a free meal every day before his shift started. A small blessing, but one that helped him save money, along with his grandmother bringing groceries over every Sunday afternoon. His mother, though perhaps stubbornly, accepted her charity, always acting civil toward her on these visits.

"Ma, you want any breakfast?" he called out as he walked by her bedroom on his way to the bathroom. She normally worked on Saturdays at the salon, but a couple of her regulars scheduled to come in on Sunday instead, her normal day off, so she traded days with a coworker. She grunted something back to him, which he assumed meant yes. Her behavior had changed in several ways recently, not just her relationship with her mother, but she also cut back on her nights at the Wagon Wheel since the incident with Randy, only going maybe three times a week as opposed to five or six.

Asher pushed the bathroom door open and a gust of mustiness greeted his nose. The room had slowly rotted for years from a water leak at the toilet and a poorly retrofitted shower that sent a constant spray of water out onto the floor. The deterioration turned the floor into a maze of where to step and where not to step, just to sit on the toilet. The only safe way he knew of to make it across the room involved knowing where the floor joists ran, so he could step somewhere without his foot sinking down through the spongy rotted subfloor hidden beneath the seventies avocado green linoleum. Sooner or later, he imagined, either he or his mother would end up sitting on the toilet in the crawlspace.

A chill ran up his leg—well, not exactly a chill—a vibration from his phone in the pocket of his shorts. He reached in and pulled it out, then squatted down to take care of his business, though hovering slightly above the seat to avoid hastening the toilet's eventual collapse.

"I need to see you," the message read. It came from Jessica. He sighed.

"When?" he texted back.

"NOW!" An immediate response informed him.

"My mom's here," he warned her.

"We'll talk on the porch," she answered.

He then replied that they could meet now, but he could not imagine what she wanted, especially with this mom there. Sex? He scrolled back through their recent messages, nothing of any urgency or interest in them anywhere since the breakup.

Ten minutes later, she stood on the front porch, staring in through the screen door. She did not knock or pound on the door to alert him but simply waited there, a frozen look on her face, until he walked into the living room and spotted her.

He pushed the screen door open. "Do you want to come inside?" he asked her.

She shook her head and walked over to the corner of the

porch and sat down in an old wicker chair. He stepped out the door and followed her, then sat on the rusty porch glider that faced her.

"I'm in trouble," she said in a low voice, tears filling her eyes.

"Trouble?" he asked, ready for her to share more details. But she only looked at him, tears now falling from her chin. "Wait," he said, now understanding the silence and the fear on her face. "A baby?" he asked.

She started to speak, but her trembling lips stopped her, so she only nodded.

"What's going on?" Bridget asked from the other side of the screen door.

Asher rushed to the door, holding it closed so his mother could not come out onto the porch with them. "We're just talking," he stammered, but could tell by the look in her eyes that she already heard enough.

"You got her pregnant, didn't you?" his mother cried out, followed by a sob and a burst of tears.

On his left, he could hear Jessica weeping. He did it; he set the course for Jessica to become his mother, and for him to follow her same failures. A father at eighteen. The hope of college and escape from the town vanished.

"Go inside and close the door," he ordered his still bawling mother. She only partly followed the order, stumbling away into the kitchen, with the inside door still wide open.

His thoughts seemed fuzzy, and he felt the pulsing throb of a vein in his right temple. "You said you were on the pill," he chided.

A loud wail escaped her, and then she quieted. "I thought I was; at least, I took what my uncle gave me," she mumbled. "I don't know what to do. My mom just glared at me, as if I was dirty and bad." She stood and paced back and forth across the length of the porch several times, standing tall as she walked, as if she were the shocked lone survivor of some horrific accident.

"You did it on purpose, didn't you?" Bridget called out, her face almost sinister as she peered out through the screen door.

A broken laugh escaped Jessica. "Like you with Tom Summer," she countered, though her face reflected what might be disbelief at her own words. A vengeful retort to an angry judgment.

Bridget's face turned white, and she receded back into the house, hiding from any additional attacks.

"I'm sorry," Jessica cried as she turned back to face him, knowing she'd crossed a line.

He'd nearly missed the angry interaction, though, as his own thoughts dwelled on his new reality. "I knew I should have used condoms, but you said the pill meant we didn't have to," Asher quietly whispered. His entire body felt weak, his entire life out of control.

"I don't think..." she started, then stopped, her face turning pale and her hands flailing against her sides. She seemed to want to say more but, at the same time, could not bring herself to say it.

A light sobbing could be heard from inside the house, his

mother no doubt hurt by the insult and probably blaming herself for her son repeating her own mistakes.

"You could get one of those procedures," he suggested.

Tears again flooded her eyes. "My mom said only whores and sluts get abortions," she countered in a harsh voice.

"What about adoption?" he asked.

"No one will want it," she angrily countered. "Not once they know about it."

What did that mean? Once they knew about it? With wobbling legs, he made his way back to the glider and slowly sat. "We'll get married," he told her. The idea frightened him, being with her every day, someone he knew he did not love, or ever would. But his child needed a father, and not only on weekends, one at home every day. Yes, he would marry her so it would have both parents together.

A weak laugh came in response, the type the exhausted or broken gave when they abandoned hope.

"I won't marry you," she coldly balked. "What a pair we would make, white trash and living in some dump. No hope of a better life, no education, grubbing for a few dollars. I can't imagine a more depressing future."

He stood, feeling a sudden jolt of confidence. "I want to take care of it; it's mine," he cried out.

"Sure," she replied in a hollow tone. "Take care of it; toss me a few dollars occasionally; let your drunk mother babysit." Jessica shook her head in disgust, as if the only life the child could possibly have would parallel the suffering and want of its father, or maybe the darkness that seemed to dwell in its mother just below the surface.

"I'll do better than that," he answered.

She stepped over to the top of the porch stairs and looked out across the yard. "How? Find a job, and drop out of school?" she asked. "And when? I already need money to see the doctor, or to do whatever else."

Money, he thought. *I have some money.* "Wait here," he told her before running into the house and to his bedroom. He opened the closet door and pulled out a small box hidden behind his clothes. In it, he counted $567, so he peeled off $250 and took it back to the porch.

"No," she protested as he handed it to her. Her eyes darted around, unwilling to meet his.

"I'll get you more," he answered, feeling a small measure of pride in helping to provide, despite the oppressiveness of the greater situation.

"It's just..." she started, but then quieted. Again, she seemed worried about sharing too much. She turned away from him, tucking the money into her pocket and quickly stepping down the porch steps. He watched as she crossed the yard, headed down the street, and finally disappeared among the trees.

How had he acted so irresponsibly? All the times they had sex and never used a condom? And why did she get birth control from her uncle? It seemed random. Why not her mother, or go to a clinic by herself? He didn't ask her how far along she was. How callous. No wonder she wanted to leave so quickly.

The sobbing from inside the house stopped. He had not checked on his mother when he went looking for the money. Now, he stood outside her closed bedroom door and knocked.

"Come in," she answered in a weak voice.

He opened the door and stepped inside to a larger room than his own, though only slightly, with his great-grandmother's gold-and-green floral wallpaper still clinging to the walls, though sagging and peeling away in random spots. "I'm sorry, Momma," he managed to whimper before collapsing on the bed beside her, tears now gushing from his eyes. She did not respond with words, only slid her arm around him and pulled him close to her. "What am I going to do?" he asked. Still, she made no sound, just gently cradled him in her arms.

For the rest of the day, Asher felt as if he were staggering through fog, his thinking muddled and his actions almost robotic as repetitive motions kept him moving. Sally asked a half dozen times what bothered him, but he gave no answer, only shrugged her off. Even cranky Sam seemed concerned, sending him home at 9:00 p.m., though dozens of dishes sat stacked in the kitchen, all in need of a run through the dishwasher. And Asher, uncharacteristically, did not argue, simply nodded and quickly left via the front door, stepping out into a midsummer evening with particularly saturating humidity.

Standing on the sidewalk in front of the diner, he pulled out his phone and sent Blaine a message. Seeing a friend would help right now. *In Springfield on a date. Be home around midnight,* Blaine responded. That would be another three hours. He took a deep breath and shook his head.

The town square sat dim and quiet, with only a few residual lights on, most noticeably at the hardware store across the park from the diner. Years past, according to his mother, the square came alive on Saturday nights, with dozens of teenagers cruising in their cars, while making intermittent stops to chat with the various cliques who hung out on the sidewalks and benches along the way. Cruising still happened in the town, but not here. Now they cruised up and down the bypass, where the fast food restaurants gave them places to stop and eat and chat. They no longer lined up in their cars in front of the courthouse steps, chatting beneath the long-stilled clock that sat perched in the eave above the building's four iconic pillars.

Asher paused at the curb in front of the diner and looked both ways, though he knew it was pointless with no traffic on the square. He took a defeated breath and trotted across the street and then onto one of the battered concrete paths that traversed the park, by way of the old bandstand. Even longer back than the cruising teenagers, concerts commonly took place in the park during the spring, summer, and fall, with the school or I.O.O.F. band melodizing from the bandstand. His late grandfather Alvin Brock told him that piece of vanished local history. The shadowy octagon-shaped bandstand now stood empty, no one cavorting or meditating within its rotting architecture, so Asher walked up the steps, each creaking loudly, and sat on the only remaining bench, as six more had at some point been ripped from the inner side of the railing.

He thought of college and how increasingly impossible it seemed. In fact, his senior year of high school also seemed to be fading. But what could he do? The chicken processing plants closer to Springfield might hire him when he turned eighteen, only a few weeks away. But he had no car to get there and less than $850, including today's paycheck, which would not buy anything trustworthy to drive. The bank account held enough money. But no, he would never touch that. He might be able to get a car for a couple thousand, not a pretty one, but maybe enough to get him to and from a job at the processing plant. How would he manage to save a couple thousand, especially with Jessica needing money for the baby? His head throbbed. How could he make it work? He leaned back against the railing and closed his eyes, starting to drift into sleep, but a noise startled him, the sound of a loud engine shutting off, followed by the slam of a car door.

CHAPTER EIGHT

"WHAT ARE YOU doing here, faggot?" an angry voice called out in Asher's direction.

He knew who said it without needing to turn around to look. Only Tommy Summer regularly favored that slur.

A pained sigh escaped Asher as he shifted on the bandstand bench to watch as his aggressor neared. Tommy strutted proudly through the overgrown trees and bushes that cluttered the park, his eyes never leaving his prey. Behind the quick-moving figure followed two slower shadows, the same two classmates from weeks earlier, obediently, if apathetically, following their alpha. It would seem unlikely that from a distance of at least fifty feet Tommy could so easily recognize his favorite target sitting late at night in a dark bandstand surround by an unlit park, but after years of prolonged antagonism, the bully had developed an almost preternatural ability to recognize Asher at a distance.

"What do you want, Tommy?" Asher yelled in response, his growing anxiety causing his body to tremble. He wanted to leap from the top of the bandstand railing and run as fast as his legs would let him. For one-on-one, Tommy outmatched him, and to-night included reinforcements.

"I came to kick your ass," Tommy threatened.

An unimaginative retort, Asher thought. *No one could ever say Tommy had wit or charm.*

"Leave me alone," Asher warned, making his voice sound as gruff as possible.

"Know what I heard, guys?" Tommy loudly announced as he circled around the front of the bandstand and the steps that led up into it. "This little faggot must go both ways because he's been bang-ing Jessica Weddle."

The two tagalongs erupted in synchronized giggles.

"Do you think about some naked dude when you do her? Maybe your buddy Blaine?" Tommy taunted.

His chance to safely flee gone, Asher stood and walked across the bandstand toward Tommy, who loomed on the top step. He approached Tommy with no intention to touch or speak, only to pass him on his way down the steps. But, as he neared Tommy, the bigger boy's open hand swung up and pushed hard against Asher's chest, sending him stumbling backward and tumbling down onto the creaking deck of the bandstand. The two observers offered another burst of laughter.

"Where are you going?" Tommy barked as he walked over to where Asher sat on the bandstand floor. Tommy then kicked Asher in the side.

"Oomph." The sound escaped Asher in response to the kick, but he held back the urge to scream. Tommy kicked again, this time hitting his arm.

"Get up," Tommy yelled.

Another kick followed, the force sending Asher rolling over onto his side. And another, this time to Asher's back, eliciting the scream he could no longer restrain. Tommy continued to kick, as Asher struggled to climb onto the bench where he had been sitting moments earlier.

"Did that hurt, faggot?" Tommy cried out.

The two shadows remained outside the bandstand, nervously glancing at each other.

The kicking stopped, and then Tommy's fist came crashing against the left side of Asher's face, but not before Asher managed a kick of his own, his foot unfortunately landing south of Tommy's groin. Tommy's face flared bright red in response to the near miss. "Alan, Jock, get up here and hold him so I can really teach him a lesson," Tommy called out to the two still waiting. They didn't move. "Now," Tommy screamed.

Alan and Jock shuffled where they stood for a moment, but neither stepped forward. "Dude, come on, he's your brother," one of them responded.

Tommy spun around to face them, his stomping feet causing the entire bandstand to shudder. "He's not my brother," he warned them, spit flying from his mouth as he did so. "His mother's some whore who tried to blame my dad. His dad could be half the men in town."

Despite a throbbing pain in his side and face, Asher took advantage of the distraction and climbed up and over the bench and leapt from the railing onto the ground.

"Get back here," Tommy roared as Asher took off in a limping run.

Asher knew Tommy would not let him go without a chase. He made it as far as the leaning World War I monument at the edge of the park before Tommy caught him. The aggressor grabbed hold of Asher's leg and pulled it out from under him, causing them both to fall to the ground beside the age-worn marble memorial.

"You made it a lot worse," Tommy hissed as he used his knee to pin Asher's legs to the ground. "I hope you want your brains bashed out against this rock."

Tommy took a tight hold of Asher's hair, then pulled his head back, aiming it for the corner of the monument. Asher prayed for help.

"Let him go, Tommy Summer," came a clear, high voice. Sally

from the diner.

"Get out of here, bitch," Tommy called back to her. But, despite the defiant tone, his grip loosened, and Asher's head dropped back to the ground.

Asher looked up, spotting Sally about fifteen feet away with a small pistol in her hand, pointed at Tommy.

"You going to shoot me, bitch?" Tommy snarled at her.

"If you make me," she calmly warned him.

The knee on top of Asher's legs disappeared, and Tommy now stood beside him, glaring at Sally.

"You wouldn't," he taunted her.

"You could have killed him, so I sure as hell would," she said. "And I'd have your own friends to get me off. Look at them way back there. They weren't going to help you."

Tommy swung around. Alan and Jock had never left the bandstand. "Wusses," Tommy growled.

Sally had dropped the hand with the gun to her side, patiently watching as Tommy stomped his way across the park to his truck, his friends slowly following.

"Can you get up all right?" she asked Asher as she neared him, the hand without the gun outstretched to give him aid.

His side and his head ached, but he had no problem getting to his feet.

"What happened?" Sally asked.

Asher shook his head. "I was sitting on the bandstand, and he saw me, so he came after me," he told her.

"Come back to the diner, and we'll talk," she responded. "I also talked to your momma a little while ago. She told me your news too."

The cold of the ice bag stung as Sally pressed it against the battered side of Asher's face. "Hold it there," she told him.

With no customers and most of the lights off, the diner had an eerie feel, as if some ghoul waited in the shadowy corners, ready to grab him and bash him against the wall. But no, Tommy did that. Asher felt lucky that Sally stayed at work late, going over the books and food orders for her father, or Tommy might have really killed him. Could he have done it? Bashed Asher's head against the monument until his body shuddered in a grim finality?

It had probably not been Tommy's initial goal—that, instead, simply being to knock him around to belittle him. But he snapped when someone used the word "brother." That single word unleashed a monster, one that might have killed, leaving a dead and bloody heap against a memorial for the dead and bloody bodies of a century earlier.

"How do you feel?" Sally asked.

"Fine," he grunted, though not really, but he knew in a day or two he would, physically anyway.

She nodded. "Want me to call the police?" she asked, then sighed. "I should have already. Someone needs to do something about that animal."

Asher shook his head. He expected little benefit in calling the police, knowing it might lead to increased ostracizing. Skepticism showed in Sally's eyes. Not calling went against her judgment.

"Your mom told me about Jessica," she said, sharply changing the conversation.

A shiver ran through his body. He did not know what to say. So he only offered a shrug in response.

"She thinks she failed you," Sally continued.

"It's not that," he replied. "I wasn't careful; now I've screwed everything up."

She put her hand on his shoulder. "I doubt you've screwed everything up," she told him.

He shook his head. "No college, and maybe I won't finish high school this next year," he argued. "I need to get a job to help take care of the baby. I don't have any money, and I can't make enough working here."

Chair legs scraped against the floor as Sally suddenly stood, looking down at him as she did so. "Lots of folks have still gone on to college after having a kid," she replied.

The impossibility of it! Sure, plenty of people went to college when they had children, but how many of them had no money and little support at home? Even before a baby showed up, his ability to go to college probably wavered at about 50 percent. Mrs. Donovan thought he should go and kept sending him scholarship forms. But her pipe dreams for him did not equate to the reality he woke up to every day.

To the uninformed outside observer, everyone had a chance to make something better of themselves. Blind faith in the American dream. If success only took hard work, why were cemeteries full of people who died in their forties and fifties after toiling away for decades on farms or in factories and other hard labor? Often, the difference between a plump, smooth-faced man in the corner office and the hunched over craggy-skinned one digging someone else's ditches did not come from hard work alone but from lucking into the right opportunities and environment to attain success. How many people did he know who had a four-year college degree, outside of his teachers at school, anyway? Less than five, he suspected. Yet, here was someone, someone who knew how hard it could be, telling him college might still happen. She knew better—she knew the moment the sperm had reached the egg weeks earlier his bright future had dimmed considerably.

"Sure, maybe," he answered, but could not look at her when doing so, feeling disingenuous in suggesting it.

"What's the girl want?" Sally asked.

He sighed. "I told her I'd marry her, but she said no without even thinking about it," he explained.

Sally nodded, seeming to have already known that answer.

"She acted so odd about it and rejected almost everything I offered her, except for the money I gave her," he continued, feeling his heart sink deep into his stomach as he said it.

Some inaudible word came from Sally, something Asher assumed was a slur against Jessica. It bothered him, as he felt a subtle need to defend the mother of his child, though he did not say anything.

Sally walked away from the table to the front of the diner, where she looked out the window and across the park. "Tommy's truck is gone," she commented. "Think you'll be okay walking home?"

The pain in his side had subsided, but his body still felt battered and achy as he stood. *It must be nearly midnight,* he thought, as he had sat out in the bandstand alone for quite a while before Tommy arrived.

"I'm good," he answered.

"Don't let your momma see your face tonight," Sally told him. "She's upset enough right now. Seeing you like this won't help."

Asher nodded. "She's not home now anyway. She worked today and is staying the night in Springfield for tomorrow's holiday," he replied.

"Independence Day," Sally offered. "I almost forgot."

He left the diner walking slowly, his body sore from Tommy's hits and kicks, the first couple blocks taking twice as long to pass. But the sight of the blue Toyota parked in his driveway gave Asher extra pep in traversing the last block to his house. Blaine sat on the top porch step, leaning back and looking up at the stars.

"Hey," Asher called out, feeling happy for the first time that day.

Blaine flashed a smile, but it vanished as a look of surprise appeared on his face. "What happened to you?" he asked.

Asher shook his head. "Tommy attacked me in the park," he explained. "Sally had to pull a gun on him to make him stop."

A gasp escaped Blaine's gaping mouth. "That's crazy," he responded after a pause. "Are you all right?"

Asher sat on the step beside him. "Sally took care of me," he answered. *Do I tell him about the rest, about Jessica?* He sighed and closed his eyes. Why couldn't he just spend time with his friend? "There's something else," he continued, then told him about the surprise pregnancy.

"Wow," Blaine commented once Asher finished. "I was surprised you ever got with her in the first place. Now this. It's so crazy."

Tears welled in Asher's eyes, making everything around him look blurry. "I don't know what to do," he said. "I feel as if everything I've wanted will never happen, no more college and moving somewhere else." A sob escaped him. Then he felt warmth, as Blaine put his arm around him and pulled him close.

"Dude, you are the smartest guy I know," his friend told him in a gentle voice. "You'll figure it out, and I'll do anything I can to help you. I'm sorry I haven't been a better friend lately. I should have jacked Tommy's jaw that day in the diner, instead of letting him talk to you that way."

The weight on Asher's heart lifted slightly. "I don't need you to protect me," he replied without irritation. "I do appreciate it though. Being around you makes me feel better. It always has, way back to the second grade."

Blaine leaned his head against Asher's. "You're going to go to college, you're going to get an awesome job somewhere, and you're going to be happy," he offered. "Lots of people go to college who have kids. It might not be easy, but if they can do it, you can."

Their heads parted, and they both leaned back as far as possible on the step while looking at each other. It didn't feel right to say anything else, but Asher wanted to lean closer to Blaine, maybe kiss him. No, not maybe. He did want to kiss him. But he wouldn't. Something inside him told him it would not be welcome.

CHAPTER NINE

ON SUNDAY MORNING, Asher called Jessica three times. She never answered, letting them all go to her voice mail. Considering her revelation to him of her pregnancy the morning before, he assumed she would want to talk to him, but no. Instead, uncertainty left his mind swirling in angst. He felt as if she wanted to make him vanish. After all, how difficult could it be to send a single text in reply? Maybe it simply had to do with it being the Fourth of July?

On a day this social, she would have a hard time avoiding him if he actively looked for her, which he planned to do. He knew once darkness arrived most of the town would gather at the high school football field to watch fireworks. And her mother's and uncle's snow-cone truck would be there with her almost certainly working the window.

Sunday also meant he had the day off, though he would have preferred to work, as it would help him escape the emotions crowding his mind, not to mention adding some cash to his pocket. Waking early and unable to go back to sleep, he had climbed out of bed at eight and mowed the lawn, despite his body feeling sore from the beating he'd suffered the previous night. A week earlier, before impending fatherhood found him, he'd lounged around in bed until nearly eleven.

The grass neatly trimmed and a trace of order now restored among the overgrown shrubbery and piles of rusty junk that polluted the yard, he stumbled into the kitchen in an achy and drowsy daze. The last of the cereal and milk slopped into his bowl; thankfully, he expected his grandmother to bring more by in late afternoon. Though, once she heard about Jessica's pregnancy, her charity might vanish, with her tossing his future onto his own mother's waste heap. He quickly finished eating, too anxious to sit at the table alone, and after rinsing his bowl, placed it in the dish rack to dry. With his future seemingly in shambles, he wanted to maintain some order and neatness.

He staggered to the bathroom, then carefully stepped across its sagging floor to turn on the hot water for a shower. Pipes clanged and vibrated inside the wall for a moment before a rush of water burst out of the showerhead. Every time he turned on the water, with the melody of disorder that sounded from behind the baby-blue tile, he imagined pipes exploding and ripping the wall open, sending a drenching downpour over him. Not today though, for following the customary clanking and clattering, a clear stream appeared. *Thank god.* He needed his shower. He needed the comfort of being clean, even with his muddled thoughts and battered body, which left him feeling more like a bruised walking husk than a human.

Refreshed, that was the cliché used to describe having a shower, but not to Asher, not today. He did feel clean, though that seemed fleeting as the old house's unmitigated humidity and heat quickly claimed him. The ramshackle cottage always felt stifling in the summer. He wiped the fog from the bathroom mirror, all while balancing his footing on the floor joists. Tommy's blows from the night prior had left surprisingly limited bruising, especially considering the number of hits he landed. Asher's face had survived with only a moderately blackened eye and a bruise on the right side of his jaw, though his torso bore more obvious remnants of the attack: four or five deep purple souvenirs.

He closed his eyes and took a deep breath, reopening them to look upon what seemed a notably less handsome face, all in the lapse of twenty-four hours. His expressive eyes looked tired and bloodshot, especially the one Tommy's fist had made contact with, now having dark smudges beneath them. And his lack of personal grooming solidified his place in the local white-trash community, as stringy peach fuzz with little dark wisps of hair crisscrossed his cheeks and chin, while a downy mustache rested on his upper lip. The look of a homeless boy.

He should shave. He knew he should but never had. A late bloomer in the facial hair department, two weeks from turning eighteen and patchy fuzz the best he could produce. Several boys younger than him at school had started shaving daily years earlier. His shaggy dark hair only worsened the effect, an overgrown hedge perched atop his well-defined face.

He toweled himself off. Why would she marry him? He had nothing to offer and no future, all while having the appearance of a vagrant. The handsome looks he occasionally got praise for buried beneath his growing insecurities. And his clothes, tattered rags. How could he feel better about himself if he looked like someone who did not care? He glanced around the bathroom, his eyes pulling toward the shower. Maybe that would work? The pink plastic razor his mother used on her legs. What about shaving cream? She had none, but he could try using soap suds.

Water poured hot from the sink faucet. He had no complaints about the old water heater. And with a surprising amount of aggression, he rubbed a wet washcloth against a bar of Ivory soap, creating a decent amount of lather, though not the foamy cream he saw on the Barbasol commercials. He dabbed the suds across his cheeks and chin and then over his upper lip. It seemed enough for his sparse collection of facial hair. Where to start? He thought for a moment, then gently pulled the razor down from the bottom of his nose to the top of his upper lip. It moved easily, mostly, with only a tinge of discomfort as it pulled at a few of the longer hairs among his soft fuzz. He continued along his entire upper lip, then moved below, dragging the razor down over his chin. Emotional growth exploded inside him as the razor cleared his feeble beard and then gratification came in from seeing the smooth sweep across his face. He moved to his right cheek and carefully sheared it, leaving a single dot of blood where he nicked a pimple. He repeated the action on his left side, but without any similar damage. For the first time that day, he smiled as he appraised his smooth face in the mirror.

Such an inconsequential thing to feel invigorated by, he thought as he dug through his closet, searching for something not completely threadbare. In a far back corner, he found a nearly new button-down shirt, one his grandmother had given him for Christmas, and then he hunted for his least scruffy pair of shorts. The shirt pulled tight against his body as he buttoned it up, making his face fall for a moment in disappointment, until he caught sight of himself in the mirror and discovered the tightness was flattering rather than unsightly.

"I'm going to feel better about myself," he said aloud as he walked across the living room, counting out $100 in cash, more than enough for a haircut, with some leftover to give Jessica so she knew he supported her. *No more wallowing. Be positive.*

Though still relatively quiet, the town square had a slight vibrancy to it this morning with patriotic bunting draped from the courthouse windows and wrapped around the streetlamps that lined Commercial Street, the avenue that ran along the southern side of the square. The annual parade, which started at 1:30 p.m., would move along that street, beginning on the grounds of the former and now empty high school, running past the square and proceeding another two miles before concluding on the football field of the new high school, where booths and other activities would take place throughout the day in advance of the town's fireworks display in the evening.

Until a few years earlier, a carnival had taken place as part of the annual Independence Day celebration, with rides, games, pageants, and competitions. But interest in it had waned and budgets decreased, so in recent years the celebration became limited to a half-dozen stalls selling food and a small tent of local crafts. Occasionally, a local band might perform for a few hours, though the attendance at those shows typically stopped at family and friends of its members. He did miss the rides, as his mother could seldom afford to take him anyplace as expensive as Silver Dollar City, so in many years they had been the only amusement rides he rode.

A handful of cars sat outside the diner—likely some folks were grabbing lunch before the parade—and a few businesses that normally closed on Sundays had their open signs out to attract the crowd, or at least what passed for a crowd, in White Oak City. The barber shop on the corner across Commercial Street from the old hotel, one of the town's most notable empty edifices, had its lights on and a red neon sign glowing, another rarity on a Sunday but lucky for Asher.

An elderly man wearing a baby-blue smock sat snoring in the barber chair, but quickly jumped to action upon hearing Asher's shoes clicking against the hexagon-tiled floor.

"What can I do for you, young man?" the barber asked as he stood up, whipping a green cape open in front of him as he did so.

Asher felt nervous coming into the shop. He could save the twelve dollars by asking his mom to cut it for him. In fact, prior to the moment he stepped inside the barbershop door, he never realized that only she had ever cut his hair.

"I...I need a haircut, please," he mumbled.

The barber nodded and pointed to the chair, which Asher quickly dropped into.

"How you want it?" the barber asked, intense blue eyes staring through the thick lenses of black-framed glasses.

"Um, short," he responded.

The man took a step back, and recognition sparked in his eyes. "How about nice and short on the sides and back, and long enough for you to comb up with a little style on top?" the barber suggested.

Asher nodded. Hopefully, the man would leave him looking remotely decent, though he felt his body tense as the first pass of the electric razor sheared off clippings that looked several inches in length. If it turned out bad, he would ask his mom to give him a buzz cut, once her routine style for him during the summer. The clippers moved quickly around Asher's head, with a series of buzzes both short and long, then the barber put the electronics away and pulled out his scissors for the top. Asher sat unmoving throughout, only adjusting the angle of his head based on the man's nudges, and not wanting to cause a mishap. After a few minutes, the scissoring stopped, followed by a few touch-up buzzes with the clippers, then a few runs of the comb through Asher's hair, cleaning out loose trimmings. He looked up into the mirror and smiled at the result. Finally, with the finesse of a magician, the barber pulled off the cape, giving it a quick and hard shake to evict any stragglers.

A sizable pile of dark hair clippings circled the chair as Asher stood. The barber gave the haircut a last discerning look and nodded. Asher stepped closer to the mirror and ran his hand through the even, short sides and up to the longer mane on top. His handsome face returned, no longer buried beneath a bramble of face fuzz and overburdened by a ragged bush perched on top of his head. In fact, wearing his tidy clothes, he looked good, maybe better than he had ever looked before. It made him smile.

"Here you go," Asher said as he handed the barber seventeen dollars, twelve for the haircut and another five for a tip, as his mother told him never to tip anyone less than five dollars. The barber nodded and seemed pleased, though another customer had just arrived, so that may have accounted for his smile.

Out on the sidewalk, the sultry heat sank back into Asher's skin, though its oppression did not dent his now improved mood.

At the end of the street, in front of the old high school, trailers and cars were lined up, as people prepared for a parade still hours away. And drifting through the air, the notes of the practicing high school band met his ears as they prepped for their march past the dozens of derelict buildings lining Commercial Street, at least until it merged onto the bypass. Across the street, he could see the bandstand, where Tommy Summer jumped him the night before, and to the left, barely visible among the unchecked growth of the park's vegetation, he could make out the monument where his head had almost been cracked open.

He glanced at the time on his phone. Too early to head to the school grounds to look for Jessica, as people would not start arriving there until after the parade. Maybe he'd take a stroll down to the old high school to peek at the parade floats.

The sun rested high in the azure sky and blazed down on him as he walked along the town's dilapidated main street. And the blinding glare of that midday light against the old bank building's massive windows left him with only an outline of the person quickly approaching him. A hand came up and gently took hold of his arm.

"Mrs. Donovan," he called out, her face now visible as she stood between him and the offending windows.

"Hello, Asher," she responded, a smile on her face. "Do you have a minute to talk?"

He nodded.

She led him across the street and half a block down, then

pushed open a door for him to enter. "It's air-conditioned in here," she told him.

They stepped inside the cluttered office of the *Decatur County Times-Gazette.* "I work here part time," she remarked as she led him across a small lobby area to a battered, old, strawberry-red vinyl couch.

Asher had never visited the newspaper office before, so his eyes explored it in a gawking fashion. A big and open space with a turned spindle chair rail divided the cozy lobby from the greater newsroom, notable for its mismatched collection of old desks and file cabinets. In one corner, a private office intruded upon the open space, and inside that room sat the old man Mrs. Donovan had introduced to him a few weeks earlier at the diner: the newspaper's publisher and editor.

The old sofa, despite its cushions being split open to reveal age-stained polyester foam, offered a surprisingly comfortable place to rest, though Asher noted while he was seated, his teacher remained standing a few feet away.

"You look very nice today," she complimented though he sensed unease in her comment.

He nodded.

A sigh then escaped her and the pleasant look on her face faded to one more serious. "This morning, someone told me Jessica Weddle is pregnant," she announced, then went silent as she stared at him with mournful eyes.

Tears quickly gathered in his own eyes, but he clenched his jaw to keep from breaking down into a burst of sobs. *Everyone already knew in barely more than twenty-four hours!* Now, his teacher, who had spent the last three years encouraging him and praising him for his potential and the opportunity to go to college, recognized that his future would be a waste.

"Yes," he whimpered, unwilling to open his mouth and trigger uncontrolled weeping.

She started to say something else, then paused for a moment. "It's not my business, but I am curious, or worried actually," she inquired—a question but without being direct in asking it.

"It's mine," he admitted, closely watching her face. He expected and, in fact, felt he deserved, to see her expression turn cold and bitter in response to her wasted efforts.

But while her bearing remained stoic, it did not waver to something more linked to despair. After a silent moment, she nodded and said, "It complicates things but doesn't end them." A modest smile returned to her face. "I still intend to see you in college," she told him.

Tears flooded his eyes and streamed down his face. *Such a child,* he thought. "I need to take care of the baby," he countered, his voice trembling.

"I can't imagine hapless Jessica Weddle with a baby," Mrs. Donovan replied in a detached tone. "She's less ready for it than you are. You've had to learn responsibility. I don't think she's been given the opportunity to be independent, to be herself. Her mother controls her, and her uncle... Well, there's something wrong with that uncle. I've always felt uncomfortable around him and the way I've seen him leer at young girls."

What an analysis, Asher thought as he listened to her. Did all teachers create psychological profiles of their students? Mrs. Donovan did always seem to know what held him back and made him fearful of the future, and here she detailed a similar assessment for Jessica. Teachers obviously saw a lot and probably could not avoid making judgments. But how often did they actually share them? Would one of them ever be honest about what they saw when they looked at Tommy Summer?

"I asked her to marry me, and she said no," he told her. "She didn't think about it, just automatically said no. She hasn't talked to me since she told me yesterday morning. I'm going to try and find her today, maybe at her mom's snow-cone truck this afternoon."

The apprehension in Mrs. Donovan's eyes shifted, going from a broader concern for him to something more akin to fear. "Be careful doing that," she warned him. "Her uncle might be around, and he... Well, he makes me uncomfortable."

Jessica seldom talked about her uncle, though he lived with her and her mother. She talked often about her mother, mostly complaining about her rules. The few times he did remember her mentioning her uncle she had sounded almost robotic, as if a reading from a script to create an idea of him, rather than describing a real person.

Back outside, with the heat of the sun pelting down, Asher felt deflated. His conversation with Mrs. Donovan, despite her intentions, stirred new unease. So, without a clear destination in his cloudy mind, he started walking, his interest in the gathering parade floats vanishing. He ambled aimlessly on the sidewalks and streets as his fractured thoughts and emotions struggled to coalesce. They all kept leading back to Jessica and her behavior—not only in the time he dated her, but also before, her often aloof behavior, but with outbursts of intensity, such as her need to have complete control during sex. Like him, she dealt with demons of insecurity, which may have driven her into the relationship with him months earlier. Driven to his level personality, his optimism, his drive to better himself? But as it became clear they did not work as a couple, whether by his ambivalence to the relationship or her hostility to it, she kept coming back, if in the least threatening ways possible. Now, a pregnancy had followed, leading him someplace capable of draining him of self-worth and maybe driving her someplace worse.

CHAPTER TEN

THE PARADE IN its cut-rate splendor passed languidly through the town—a dwindling spectacle, or so it seemed to Asher in his review of having watched it every year for the last decade and a half. Of course, conventional wisdom says everything seems to become smaller as you age, from childhood homes to the local parade. Had it always been so paltry? Made up of a meager half-dozen floats, a handful of antique cars, an exhausted school band, and the dwindling ranks of local fraternal organizations, and only five members of the VFW marched, two of them drunkenly stumbling along.

He watched from the sidewalk in front of the old bank, alongside a couple of school acquaintances, not friends really, more the occasional student he might randomly sit next to in the school cafeteria. In addition to Blaine, he only had two close friends, despite having known most of his classmates since the first grade. And both of them happened to be girls, which caused him to hesitate to talk about Jessica's pregnancy. Would their bond as women automatically leave him with the blame?

As the end of the parade staggered by on the way down the street, his small group followed, heading in the direction of the high school grounds. He needed to head that way too, but he spotted his grandmother among a group of older women, all sitting in lawn chairs in the grass on the south end of the park. He told the others he would see them later, which they silently acknowledged before continuing on their way.

Evie Brock waved as he crossed the street headed toward her. Then her eyes narrowed as she caught sight of his blackened eye and bruised cheek. They chatted for a few minutes, with her offering only a passing comment on the marks on his face and saying nothing about his impeding fatherhood, despite the fact she already knew. His mother had called her within minutes of finding out herself, sobbing about her failure as a parent and repeating the cycle she'd started.

The grass offered a comforting softness as he settled down on it beside her lawn chair. Hundreds of times in his life, he'd nestled on grassy lawns beside his grandmother, and same as all those occasions before, it still gave him a feeling of security. He listened as the old women chatted and gossiped, offering no input of his own.

Occasionally, one of them would look at him with a sympathetic smile. They all knew his life story and had probably gossiped about it many times over the years. Even his grandmother had likely complained about her failing as a mother, maybe touching on the disgrace of having a bastard grandson. A shame his recent actions recreated for her.

"You look good with your shave and haircut," Evie said as she stood, ready to fold her lawn chair and head home for the afternoon.

Asher nodded.

She handed him the chair to carry to the car, then led the way down the block to it. "I don't know what to say about the business with this girl," she finally remarked once they reached the car, a safe distance from the rest of the departing brood.

Tears bubbled up and dripped down his cheeks. He had cried more in the last twenty-four hours than the past year. "I'm sorry," he mumbled.

She slipped her arm around him and pulled him in close for a hug. "We'll figure something out," she assured him, a comforting smile on her face.

He opened the car trunk and put the folding chair inside, carefully placing it so it would not rattle on his grandmother's drive home. He then shut the lid and stepped back onto the sidewalk. Her arm poked out of the driver's window and she offered a brief wave before pulling away. No verbal goodbye, which she seldom did. He watched as her car made its way around the north and east sides of the square, then disappeared in the direction of her home. *At least he had family.* But so had his mother.

The town square reverted to its normal deserted weekend traffic, the sidewalks empty and only a handful of cars remaining. The diner closed its doors for the rest of the day, everyone off for the holiday. His friends had left, gone off to the school grounds or somewhere else to waste time. He could go searching for Jessica, but the interaction with his grandmother, despite being so brief, had left him feeling drained and unsure of what he would say to her. Home and television, some time to reassess, he decided. Then, maybe around eight p.m., he would head over to the football field to see if he could talk to her.

Being home, with the sweltering heat and distracting silence, not even a clock ticking in the background, aggravated his exhaustion rather than alleviated it. He thought about pouring himself a bowl of cereal, but remembered he had eaten the last of it in the morning. There must be something to keep him occupied, he thought as he paced around the house, restlessness usurping his exhaustion. He could go outside and walk, and with no air-conditioning inside, the outside might be more pleasant. But he could think of nowhere to go. He texted Blaine but knew there was a new girl involved, so he didn't expect a quick response. What would have happened if he had kissed him the night before? Probably nothing good—he knew Blaine cared about him, but not like that.

He could not talk to his mother, as she'd stayed with a friend in Springfield the night before with plans to spend the day there enjoying the holiday with coworkers before watching that city's fireworks. Springfield's annual display dwarfed that of White Oak City by an absurd measure. Two years earlier, she took him there to see it, and he'd noted the fireworks lasted close to thirty minutes. The local ones lasted ten minutes at most, a small town's humble attempt at excitement.

He dropped onto the sofa and turned on the television, aimlessly flipping through the channels, paying no attention to the programs passing by with each click. His body twitched and fidgeted. What did it mean? Nervous, nervous about the baby, nervous about his life, nervous about doing exactly what his mother made him promise a dozen times not to do—make the same mistakes she had.

The turmoil in his mind slowly abated, and he drifted off to sleep as some remake of a remake played on the television. Hours passed before he finally woke in the groggy daze of incomplete sleep. The room had dimmed as the sun outside neared the horizon. *Jessica*, he thought, then jumped to his feet in response, wide awake and feeling a resurgence of need to talk to her. He pulled his phone out of his shorts' pocket. Maybe she'd texted him or called, but nothing showed on the screen, and the time neared 8:30 p.m. The fireworks started in half an hour. He realized he'd slept for nearly five hours, his body's attempt to excise his stress. He dashed to the bathroom, cautious as always about the floor, then he washed his face, brushed his teeth, and tidied his hair.

The neighbor's bicycle would get him there the fastest, but it did not rest in its usual place, so he took off on foot, jogging, but trying not to wear himself out too quickly. His years of running track had taught him how quickly one could become fatigued by starting too fast, which suddenly seemed a metaphor for his mother's life—and possibly his as well. He crossed the railroad tracks, so another mile to the high school. Cars and a few groups of walkers headed the same way but with less urgency than his. The heat clawed at him, his breathing grew heavy, and sweat left his forehead slick and shiny. The shave and new haircut would not impress anyone when paired with a reddened and sweat-streaked face.

Almost there, and though his shirt felt as if a wet paper towel wrapped around his body, he could not help that right now. Maybe once the sun finally disappeared into the night, he could cool down enough to dry out. He jogged past the dozen or so booths and trucks lined up at the northern end of the football field, the last of them being a faded yellow truck—the one that sold snow cones. He slowed as he neared and walked a cautious arc away from the serving window. Jessica's mom stood behind it, oblivious to his presence as she took cash and handed out treats to her line of customers. Back behind her, the uncle scooped up shaved ice and poured on syrup. No sign of Jessica.

Asher ducked back behind the yellow truck, hoping without

reason to find her there, but no. He sighed. Maybe she skipped the celebration, if only to avoid him. A few hundred people had gathered on the football field, many stretched out on blankets laid over the grass, locals relaxing until the show started. He walked among them, his eyes darting everywhere in search of her and feeling clumsy and conspicuous as he did so. Several people he knew said hello. He replied in kind, though he kept moving to avoid any prolonged conversation. As it hit 9:00 p.m., a loud blast of recorded patriotic music began playing, an uneven mix of John Phillip Sousa and Toby Keith. *Who came up with that?* Two genres with a century between them and nothing to soften the transition.

The deafening cracking and popping started, quickly followed by bursts of color in the sky above the crowd, who replied in expected oohs and aahs. The rockets went up fast, three or four bright explosions at a time, most modest in size, but a couple bigger dollar investments as well, which accordingly received the loudest gasps of appreciation. *Pop, pop, pop,* and then nothing—the music still played, but the explosions ceased. Then the music abruptly stopped halfway through some new all-American anthem no one would remember the next year. The mayor's voice came over the loudspeaker, thanking everyone for attending and telling them to have a safe trip home. Asher pulled out his phone. It read 9:09 p.m. The entire show, including the musical interlude, had lasted less than ten minutes. Except for his need to find Jessica, the show did not feel worth it to leave the house.

He started walking again, hoping to spot her. Most of the attendees hurried, gathering their blankets and lawn chairs, then dashing to their cars, their children running with them. At the end of the field, he could hear the vendors making final pitches to the evaporating crowd. In the snow cone truck, he still only made out Jessica's mother and uncle. He turned toward the south end of the field and saw a small group, well illuminated against the dark tree line behind them. In the center of the group stood the person he came to find.

"Jessica," he called out as he ran toward her. She glared at him, her expression almost fearful. A few of her friends stood beside her. He knew them all and nodded in greeting, but not one responded in kind, only staring at him in response.

"Can we talk?" he asked her. She glanced to her friends, as if seeking guidance, then pointed toward a slight opening in the trees, out of view from the opposite end of the field. He walked to the spot and waited for her as she took a moment to talk to her friends, which she followed by taking a long drink from a bottle.

"What is it?" she asked in a cold voice as she neared him.

The bluntness stung him. He expected some sort of recognition or appreciation for trying to be involved.

"I wanted to make sure you're okay and see if you needed anything," he replied in a soft tone.

A sigh escaped her, as did the noticeable odor of alcohol. "I'm fine," she mumbled.

He reached into his pocket and pulled out $300, rolled up tightly. "I have this; it'll help you buy stuff for the baby or the doctor," he offered.

Tears welled up in her eyes. "No," she protested. "I shouldn't have taken the money from you yesterday either."

A new ache throbbed in his stomach. "I am going to take care of my baby," he insisted, holding the money back out toward her. Again, she refused.

She shook her head. "You don't understand," she quietly whimpered, tears now in her eyes.

"Marry me," he asked.

The tears spilled out and trickled down her cheeks. "Is that why you shaved and got a haircut?" she asked.

Did it really come across that obvious? "I'm a man, and I'm going to do everything I can to help you," he proclaimed though his voice wavered.

"I don't love you," she countered.

While he knew he did not love her either, it still hurt. It hurt more than he expected, causing tears to flood his own eyes.

"But the baby," he whispered almost silently.

Jessica shook her head, which she followed by taking another long drink from the bottle.

"Is that alcohol?" he asked.

She nodded.

"That's bad for the baby," he warned, his strength growing with his new concern.

A gasp escaped her. A sound of guilt mixed with fear and uncertainty.

"Can I talk to your mom?" he asked.

"No," she angrily shot back. "She doesn't know about you. She doesn't care who the father is. She—I don't know—she's confusing me about it." Another drink followed. "I'm sorry, Asher. You're nice and sweet and handsome. I'm sorry I told you about it. I don't want you to worry. My mom says we'll take care of it; we'll do what's right." A sob escaped her.

"But, if you..." He started, knowing she meant the possibility of abortion, but she cut him off.

"No, no, no," she warned him. "You have enough problems. I shouldn't have told you. I just did because I needed someone to care about me or feel sorry for me."

Asher gently put his hand on her arm. "I do care. I'll do anything I can," he offered. "And you can't mean an abortion. You told me what your mom said about girls that have those."

Jessica's face went pale. "She said it's okay in this case, because we don't know..." she started but then stopped and pulled away from him, stepping back in the direction of her friends. "Stop calling and texting me," she warned him. "It'll get me in trouble."

Once she reached her group, they took off running across the football field, none looking back to see if he followed. Should he go after her? In an old movie, the hero would, but he knew at this moment that type of gesture would not help. Instead, he remained standing where she'd left him, just inside the tree line, defeated and concealed by the evening's darkness. Did she mean it when she said she did not want him involved? He would not repeat the actions of his own father, a coward hiding in plain sight. He turned and stepped deeper into the woods.

Weeds and brambles swatted at his legs as he walked away from the lights and voices. Somewhere in this stand of second growth forest stood an old barn, and though the darkness made it difficult to see more than a few feet ahead, he knew the direction to follow to find it. The undergrowth grew thicker, pulling at his socks and shorts; then as he ascended a gradual hill, the trees and brush cleared to reveal a lumbering structure some forty feet high. Light from the half-moon streamed down over the tops of the trees, offering enough illumination for him to make his way around the building without tripping or falling. A side door stood ajar, so he pulled it open and stepped inside a long room lined with broken wooden stanchions, the barn's former milking parlor.

Inside the old barn, itself surrounded by a cooling cocoon of trees, in the early hours of the night, the oppressive summer heat and humidity abated. He leaned against a massive oak post that rose up the entire height of the ancient building, a place to rest as he went over what Jessica said. He felt stuck in an unwinnable limbo. She claimed not to want him involved. An easy answer for him. He could go to college and create a more fulfilling life for himself. But it mirrored the cycle his own father started. Abandoning a child based on the influence of others, ignoring one's responsibility. No, Asher would not repeat that callous act.

The sound of bodies running through the woods cut through his thoughts. Cheerful and excited voices trailed in from outside. Asher walked over and cautiously peered out of the open entrance, spotting the playful wrestling of shadows some fifteen feet away.

"Who's there?" a voice called out, followed by five shadows clearly emerging from the rough play. A boy's voice, or at least a teenager, and one familiar.

"Asher Brock," he called out to them, feeling no reason to hide.

"Oh," someone muttered, and then they came closer, unthreatening in their behavior. The moonlight hit their faces and revealed them, three upcoming sophomores and two juniors, all boys. He knew them from school and was friendly with two of them.

"Are you out here by yourself?" one asked.

"Yeah," Asher replied.

"Smoking pot?" one asked, the youngest of the group. "Can we have some?"

Asher shook his head. "Nah. After the fireworks, I wanted to take a walk," he told them.

They all looked as though they didn't care.

"What are you doing out here?" Asher asked.

The boys giggled in unison.

"We have bottle rockets and stuff to set off," one admitted. Then, as if prompted to prove it, another one set off a roman candle, sending colored balls of fire up into the sky. He then aimed the firework at his friends, who scurried for safety. As did Asher, ducking back inside the barn.

"You guys are crazy," Asher yelled out, which brought on a round of laughter. From the safety of the decayed milking parlor, he watched while the five chased after each other, lighting and tossing firecrackers and targeting each other with bottle rockets. He almost wanted to join in, but he had no explosives to add to the mix and still harbored a lingering apathy toward anything fun following his conversation with Jessica.

The boys dodged in and out of the old barn, with the bursts of roman candles and bottle rockets knocking against the weathered oak plank walls. Maybe he should leave, Asher thought, instead of being stuck in the middle if they accidentally set the place on fire. With a slight wave of goodbye to one of the boys, he ran back into the woods and headed toward the high school grounds.

Nothing remained of the holiday's events when Asher reemerged onto the football field. All the viewers had disappeared and the vendors, too, leaving only a scattering of trash across the green turf to hint at the celebration of an hour or so earlier. Behind him, in the woods, the crack of bottle rockets continued, while in front of him, popping up sporadically across the town's neighborhoods, occasional sprays of fiery color appeared, despite a well-known ban on the use of fireworks inside the city limits. He crossed the football field and walked along the shoulder of the bypass, then crossed over onto Commercial Street where the old road split off toward the town square. Nothing remained open, and only a few cars passed as he walked.

He crossed the railroad tracks and looked up at the old feed mill building, which stood tall and battered. Two weeks earlier, the newspaper reported that the building, which had not housed an actual operating business in some forty years, had reached its end with demolition scheduled to start the next month. Decades ago, his grandfather had worked there, before he married his grandmother and took over her parent's farm. Asher would miss seeing the old mill and grieved for the loss of a connection to his grandfather, who still clung to his earliest memories.

His house sat shrouded in darkness as he returned to it. In his rush to get to the fireworks, he'd forgotten to turn on the porch light. Luckily, despite it being the poor part of town, seldom did he have reason to worry about his safety at night, as half the houses sat abandoned, and he knew everyone who lived in the rest. He climbed the steps to the porch and pulled out his key, but a shuffling to his left gave him pause. He slowly turned in that direction and saw a dark figure sitting there. The outline of Tommy Summer made his body shiver. "Hi, Asher," the shape spoke. Not Tommy, but Tom Summer.

"What are you doing here?" Asher asked. His body ached

with exhaustion, and he had no interest in talking to anyone right now, especially Tom Summer, the town's most infamous father.

"I-I wanted to see if you're all right," Tom answered as he stood. He had waited for him by sitting in an old rusted clamshell lawn chair, another hand-me-down from Asher's great-grandmother.

Asher did not respond, instead only staring at the man, looking into a face rendered featureless by the darkness.

"I...well...I heard Tommy hurt you, and I needed to make sure—" Tom started.

"I'm fine," Asher interrupted. "It doesn't impact you either way."

Tom stepped closer, his face now recognizable in the glare of a distant streetlight. Tears glistened in his eyes, and his hand reached toward Asher, but the teenager brushed it away as he hurried to open the front door.

"Wait," Tom called out, but Asher ignored the plea by rushing into the house and slamming the door closed behind him.

For a moment, as he stood in the hot, dark living room, Asher felt relief. Then, as he remembered the money in the bank account, his body trembled with anger, so he flipped around and jerked the door back open. "I want to know about the money," he yelled out across the porch. Tom had nearly reached his truck, which sat parked out on the street but turned and started back toward the house.

"What money?" Tom asked as he neared the porch.

Why did he say anything, Asher thought. Tom Summer had left, on his way to his truck and then wherever he came from, but now he hurriedly approached, seeming almost happy about it.

"The money in the bank—the $30,000," Asher barked in reply.

Tom paused, but only for a second, then stepped onto the bottom porch step. "That's for you," he offered. "I've been putting it in there for you since you were little."

Since he was little. Exactly what every little boy needs, money secreted away for him instead of an involved parent. "I don't want it," Asher warned, keeping behind the closed screen door, a symbolic if flimsy barrier.

"Use it for college," Tom responded. "You're smart, probably going to be valedictorian. It should help you go to a good school." The man moved up two more steps but then went back down one, perhaps seeing the anger in Asher's eyes.

"I don't want it," Asher repeated.

"I know your mom can't help you with college," Tom pressed.

"Shut up about my mom," Asher growled.

Tom took another step down. "I'm sorry; you're right," he offered with his gaze dropping to the ground. "But the money is for you, and I'm going to keep putting more in, so you can use it."

A dozen angry and bitter words bubbled up in Asher's throat, but he would not use them. He stepped back into the inky shadows of the living room and slammed the door shut. After a deep breath to calm himself, he leaned against the door, pressing his ear to it and straining to hear to the sound of Tom's footsteps as they moved away from the house and to his truck.

The roar of the pickup's engine faded into the night. Now, feeling safely alone, Asher turned on the living room light. The brightness hit his eyes while the ever-present mustiness flooded his nose. How could a house that he constantly cleaned still manage to reek of the invasive odor? One day he would live in a modern climate-controlled home and not suffer in stifling and moldy misery every summer.

He flicked on the bathroom light and pulled off his shirt. The bruising on his side had faded to yellow with only a couple spots of dark mottling remaining. Tommy Summer got to have a father, so why did he need to play the role of the angry tormenter?

Asher ran his hand down his chest and stomach, smearing sweat across his smooth skin. Not a single hair from his neck down to his waist. If not for muscle definition, he would have the body of a ten-year-old. Most of the other boys at school had at least some hair on their stomach or chest, but not him. When he stole glances at them, he sometimes wished he had been gifted with that symbol of masculinity, though his looks more often were simply ones of desire.

He turned off the bathroom light and made his way to his bedroom, where he clicked on the rattling box fan, which he had brought in from the living room, and dropped down onto his bed. Reclining back against the pile of pillows he kept pushed up against the headboard, he noticed the large yellow envelope on his nightstand. Inside it resided a vision of hope, though one now dependent on what happened with the baby. It held a dozen or so scholarship and admissions applications given to him by Mrs. Donovan. He picked it up and pulled out the stack of papers, absently thumbing through them after he did so.

Most offered money available for use at any accredited school he chose, but he knew the real prize she included among them came in the form of one of the college applications, already partially filled out. The University of Missouri, Mrs. Donovan's own alma mater, and the school she most often mentioned to him. He flipped through the pile until he found it and pulled it free of the rest. Clipped to the back, he found a second form, a scholarship application for a near-full ride. With that, Tom Summer's money would be nearly worthless, at least for Asher's most prominent goal. Like the college application, the one for the scholarship also came to him with all the basics neatly filled in, and a few easy to follow sticky notes that gave him direction on what he still needed to do, such as writing an essay and including the type of personal family information his teacher either did not know or would not feel comfortable listing for him, such as the name of his father.

He let his body relax into the pillows and closed his eyes for a moment. All the complications currently clouding his life swirled quickly through his mind. What did it hurt? He might as well apply, both for the school and the scholarship. If something happened, even if he got accepted or won the scholarship, he could always turn it down. No reason to kill his future when he did not have the present figured out.

CHAPTER ELEVEN

"DID YOU WATCH the fireworks?" Bridget Brock asked her son as she stood in the doorway of his bedroom, looking down on him as he lay stretched out on top of the covers of his bed. She wore cutoff jeans with an American flag top, so he assumed they were the clothes she'd worn yesterday. The bags under her eyes implied she had gotten little sleep overnight.

"Yeah," he mumbled, blinking himself awake. He stretched out his arms and yawned. "How was your night?" he asked.

A tired and melancholy smile emerged on her face. He knew it well. The ongoing symbol of her disappointment with life. "All right," she answered. "Me and the girls went to see the fireworks, then went dancing after that." She paused a moment. "It's not as fun as it used to be," she added. The smile faded, leaving her looking more apathetic than sad.

"You got to see better fireworks, at least," he offered. "They didn't last ten minutes here."

She sighed. "I should have brought you up to see them in Springfield with me," she replied. "We could have gone out for dinner."

Asher did not answer. He did not know how to tell her he also wished she had done that. He knew it would upset her.

"What are these?" she asked as she stepped around the side of his bed. She reached down to the nightstand and picked up the University of Missouri application. "Is this where you want to go?"

He reached over and gently pulled the application out of her hand. "Maybe," he answered. "But I don't have to turn it in until November."

Another sigh escaped her, then she sat on the edge of his bed. "Have you talked to that girl?" she asked.

The question he least wanted to answer. "I saw her last night," he replied. "She said her mom doesn't care who the father is, and they don't want me involved."

Bridget's face relaxed. "You think she means it?" she questioned.

Asher shrugged his shoulders.

"You could still go to college," his mother offered, a slight smile forming at the edges of her mouth.

"What about the baby?" he protested, his voice edgy.

"It'll be fine; you need to take care of yourself," she told him.

The remark made his body go rigid. "Same as my father did," he shot back. For the first time in years, he genuinely felt angry with his mother.

Her jaw dropped. "Not like that," she whimpered as tears came to her eyes.

"He was here last night," Asher continued, his voice steady but not kind.

"Who?" she asked in a hollow voice.

"Tom Summer," he replied. "He heard Tommy beat me up and wanted to make sure I was okay. I told him I was. I also told him I didn't need his $30,000." He spoke every word bluntly with the singular purpose of hurting her.

"You know about the money," she muttered.

"Yeah. So do you, evidently," he commented, surprised by how much she held back from him.

"It's for your college," she countered.

He crawled to the side of the bed and huddled up against her. "I don't want his money," he growled.

An exhausted groan escaped her as she stood. "I'll make waffles. I haven't done that in a long time," she passively remarked as she walked to the doorway. There, she paused and turned back to face him. "How long have you known it was him?"

The masquerade of nearly eighteen years finally ended. "Since the second grade," he answered.

Years had passed since breakfast at home meant more than cold cereal. Even during his younger years, having anything beyond the factory-produced contents of a colorful box proved rare, with his mother doing something more elaborate maybe once every other month. But, this morning, as if to prove a point or to offer an apology for her more than decade-long silence on her son's paternity, she hustled around the kitchen, digging up from some hidden place in her memory a recipe for making waffles. *Would the old waffle iron still work?* He dug it out of the storage closet in the laundry room and plugged it in near the stovetop. A little light flashed on, and he felt it beginning to heat.

"Make me some coffee, honey," she asked him. A common request on the rare mornings both found themselves at home together. He turned on the coffeemaker and pulled out a large can of generic coffee from the cabinet beside the refrigerator.

"Grandma doesn't like the taste of this brand," he remarked before dumping a couple scoops worth into the filter.

"Grandma doesn't buy it, so her opinion doesn't matter," she replied.

Indeed, his grandmother did not buy the coffee. While she supplied most of the other groceries, she never bought coffee. Because she knew Asher did not drink it, only his mother did.

The coffee brewing, he sat at the kitchen table and watched as his mom buzzed back and forth. At one point, she stopped, realizing they did not have any syrup, but quickly recovered with apples and sugar, frying them up to put on top of the waffles.

"Did you ever want to go to college?" he asked as he watched her work. A basic question, but one with an answer he'd never previously sought.

"I wanted to be a nurse," she offered, flashing him a smile steeped in nostalgia. "I did well in science and always enjoyed being around people. Maybe that's why I'm so popular at the shop?"

It made sense. Despite the apathy her disappointing life had created in her, she still wanted to take care of others, and took it hard when she either failed or misjudged in doing so, both of which often applied to her care of him.

"Why didn't you?" he asked, knowing the answer.

She paused. "I needed to take care of you," she replied, no smile this time.

"Tom Summer could have given you more money, so you could have done both," he remarked.

Bridget shook her head. "Back then he didn't have any," she explained. "It all came from her. He didn't start making his own money, at least enough to set aside some for you, until later."

An excuse. "He's a coward," Asher responded.

"Yes," she agreed but then went silent as if afraid of betraying some private agreement.

The waffles, topped with fried apples, arrived plated and steaming on the table in front of him. She had shifted, if only momentarily, into June Cleaver mode. "They're really good," he offered in praise after savoring his first bite. He meant it. Despite how seldom it occurred, and increasingly seldom in recent years, she always knew how to cook. A skill too often hidden by her personal disenchantment.

"I need to do it more often," she told him. "You'll be gone soon, and I haven't done enough of this type of thing for you."

Asher shook his head. "You don't need to worry about that," he replied. "You have work, and you're busy with other things."

Tears flooded her eyes, a couple of big drops trickling down her cheek. "I should be busy with you," she whispered in a shaky voice.

He laid his fork on the plate and stood, wrapping his arms tightly around her once he did so. "It's okay," he told her. She did not say "no" but made her disagreement known by uneasily shaking her head.

Had something about her and their home changed in the course of a morning? Or did it amount to only the built-up exhaustion of the last few days? The coming baby and his mother's regrets in not preventing a second generation of teenage pregnancy. Maybe the verbal confirmation that he knew the identity of his own father tore away the last of some barrier between them that had existed since his birth. Would this burgeoning new dynamic become something permanent? Had some fundamental aspect changed that would alter their relationship and help bring her some contentment?

Back in his chair, with his fork in hand, he shyly watched her as she ate her own breakfast, taking dainty bites as always. Her eyes wandered the room as they sat at the table together, as if looking for some escape from their more aware reality. Similar to how he never asked her to name his father, he also never asked her why she'd kept him instead of getting an abortion or putting him up for adoption. There must be a reason, perhaps the most obvious—that she could not part with her baby—or maybe something else, a sense of pride that would refuse to let Tom Summer's wife win. Sure, the wife got the man, but not without a walking, living reminder right in her hometown that her husband had another son, one better-looking and more intelligent than her own.

CHAPTER TWELVE

DOZENS OF PARKED cars crowded around the isolated farmhouse, along its rutted driveway, in the overgrown yard, and down the hill by the gray and leaning barn. Clusters of teenagers and the occasional out-of-place twentysomething ebbed and flowed between the vehicles, greeting and chatting with each other with some taking a few moments to sit on a hood and really talk. The house itself, an abandoned relic, thumped in the night air with music blasting and light blazing from its open and missing windows.

Asher typically hated these stereotypical adolescent gatherings as his introverted nature preferred socializing with a small group of friends. But weeks had passed since July fourth, and Jessica continued to ignore his calls and texts, as infrequent as he tried to make them. He knew her well enough to know she would not pass up this party. Because unlike him, the more people around, the more at ease she seemed. A voice called his name as he climbed out of Blaine's car, parked in the field beside the barn. Blaine came to most of these parties, as unlike Asher, he seemed to have fully embraced the rural teenager life. Asher glanced around but in the darkness could not tell who had called out his name.

They started up the hill toward the house, pausing when another and distinctly different voice called out to him. He looked around again, hoping to spot his second greeter, but nothing, so he nodded in the direction from which he thought the voice came. Nearing the house, he turned to his right to make a comment to Blaine, but he no longer followed, having stopped several feet back to talk to a pretty girl. She was unfamiliar to Asher, maybe a relative of someone. Yeah, that kiss would have been a bad idea.

Half-rotted steps creaked under Asher's weight as he made his way up onto the back porch, itself overcrowded with teenagers, several of whom he knew from school. He offered a few hellos and then stepped inside the back door, wondering as he did so what would happen if the sagging porch decided to give way under the 1,500 pounds of excess weight the partygoers forced upon it. Inside, he discovered rooms full of people but largely sans furniture, most of it probably hauled away with the last resident decades earlier. Two folding tables supported a half-dozen kegs, and with the electricity long ago shut off, dozens of camp lanterns kept the place lit while battery-powered stereos blared a warring onslaught of pop and dance music.

He moved attentively from room to room, looking for either Jessica or some of her friends who might lead him to her. About a quarter of the attendees looked familiar, either from his school or one of the neighboring districts. He spotted a T-shirt from a high school in Springfield, meaning the urbanites, or at least what passed for urbanites in the Ozarks, decided to slum it out in the boonies for a night.

Several sets of eyes followed him as he made his way through the gathering. Not in suspicion, more from a primal interest. With eyes wide and mouths slightly agape, the leering partygoers wore expressions both intense and shallow. Had he heightened his personal appeal that much with such a limited upgrade in his own hygiene—shaving and fixing his hair? Most of his admirers were female and strangers to him, though he caught a couple of boys offering similar gazes, the realization of which caused his face to flush and his stomach to flutter with anxiety.

"What are you doing here, faggot?" a familiar voice barked.

Asher's body tensed. One of the boys, one whose eyes had lingered on him longer than most, appeared to cower in response to the slur.

"Leave me alone, Tommy," Asher growled as he turned to face him.

Tommy's face darkened. "I do what I want," he warned. "And

you better stop crying to my dad to protect you, bastard."

Tom Summer's interference had only made the matter worse, as Asher suspected it would.

"I didn't ask your dad to do anything, except stay away from me," Asher responded, realizing that saying it seemed to confirm the rumors about his parentage for everyone listening.

"I'm going to hurt you bad," Tommy cried out before lunging toward Asher, but he stopped short, just as Asher crouched back to brace himself for the attack.

"Back off." Blaine's voice boomed.

Asher watched as Blaine stepped through the surrounding crowd and calmly strode up to Tommy. It made him uncomfortable seeing his friend protect him, but it also felt good knowing he cared.

"Are you worried I'll hurt your boyfriend, Blaine?" Tommy responded with a snicker.

Blaine stepped closer to Tommy, leaving about six inches between them. "I think you're leaving for the night," he informed him.

For a second, Tommy puffed up, as if ready to deliver a protest. But, he looked around the room, and stepped back, as if sensing taking on the popular Blaine might not do much for his reputation.

The threat gone, Blaine put his arm around Asher's shoulders and led him to a keg for a beer.

"Thanks for that," Asher offered before taking a short sip of beer. He had only drunk alcohol three or four times before and found the taste of beer undesirable.

"Anything for you," Blaine replied with a wide smile. "I don't know why Tommy acts that way. Jealousy maybe, and his mom's a total bitch."

Asher shrugged his shoulders. He hadn't told Blaine the real reason he came to the party with him, as he suspected his friend would have protested.

"Did you see Jessica anywhere?" Asher asked him.

An uncomfortable look appeared on Blaine's face. "I didn't think she wanted to talk to you," he replied.

Asher shrugged. "I'm going to be a father for my kid," he explained.

"She's on the front porch," he told him, shaking his head.

As was common of many old farmhouses, this one had two front doors, each leading onto the front porch from one of the two rooms on the north-facing side of the house. Asher exited from the door in the larger room, a room that at one time might have been referred to as the front parlor.

Dozens more teenagers and young adults crowded the ramshackle porch, which noticeably sagged in one corner, a structural defect that none of those standing on it seemed to worry over. He squeezed past the mass of bodies that clogged the narrow space until he spotted Jessica, leaning back against a grayed and rotted corner post, with her usual group of friends surrounding her. He had known most of this small group of teens his entire life, considering nearly everyone a friend. But in the last few weeks, they had become distant to him, as if out of respect for her. He timidly approached them.

"Hi, Jessica," he offered a quiet greeting as he neared her.

She replied with a weak smile while her group of friends parted slightly for his approach.

He silently nodded to them as he joined their group.

"How are you feeling?" he asked in a raspy voice.

Tears glistened in her eyes. "I'm fine," she replied in a forced voice and followed by taking a swig of beer.

"Should you be doing that?" he asked.

"You asked me that at the fireworks, and I told you it's none of your business," she growled in reply, though the fragile look in her eyes contradicted the harshness.

"I'm sorry. You're right," he offered though he did not feel that way. His baby deserved better. He shuffled his feet, not knowing what to avoid saying. "Mrs. Donovan sent me a bunch of college stuff," he finally said, thinking the topic out of place but the least controversial one he could offer.

"That's good," she replied in little more than a whisper. Tears continued to brim in her eyes, almost ready to spill over. "You're smart. You'll do great at college. I wish I had something to look forward to."

The words hit his ears as a plea, a cry for affirmation. "You're brilliant," he told her. "What do you want to do? I'm sure there's some way you can do it, whatever it is."

She turned her back to him, looking off into the night while grasping hold of the porch rail with both her hands. "I want to get away from my uncle, and my mom," she cried out. "That's what I want to do."

Asher stepped up beside her, following her gaze out across the yard and into the dark fields beyond. "I wish I could help," he told her.

She shook her head, and he heard a sniffle. "You're the only one who's trying to," she replied.

How could that be true? He had done so little. He had asked her to marry him, which she rejected without thinking about it. He gave her some money, which she later told him she shouldn't have taken. And he kept bugging her when she kept telling him to go away. His actions seemed disappointing or clingy, not helpful.

"I am. It's my baby," he responded, his voice little more than a mumble.

A sob escaped her. "You sure about that?" she cried.

What did she mean? They had dated, and every few days she came over, and they had sex. Did she mean it could be someone else's? Had she been seeing another boy? His breath rushed out and he felt dizzy. He grabbed hold of the porch rail to keep himself steady, but it instantly went from firm to limp, falling away from his hand. For a moment, he almost went with it but managed to balance himself and keep standing. But Jessica had screamed, and he looked down from the porch to see her sprawled on the ground below, the remnants of broken railing scattered beside her. Whereas he managed to stay upright when the rotted wood broke and crumbled, she went tumbling down onto the hard, rocky earth.

A chorus of gasps sounded around him. He leaped down and crouched to gently touch Jessica's face, but her eyes remained closed. He took her hand in his and leaned close to her ear. "Wake up," he whispered to her, and her eyes fluttered open.

"Are you okay? Can you speak?" he asked her. Dozens of others gathered around them, both on the ground and looking down from the porch.

She nodded, then her whole body shivered. "I hurt. I think it's the baby," she cried. She held her abdomen with her free hand, while a spot of blood appeared on her shorts.

"It's going to be okay," Asher told her as he continued to keep hold of her hand. His stomach heaved with uncertainty and fear. He repeated the phrase to her over and over until a hand touched his shoulder.

"We have a car to take her to the hospital," someone told him. He looked at the crowd around them, a bunch of blurred faces, then sat back and watched as they lifted her, pulling her free of his hands. She cried out in pain as they carried her. He stood and stumbled after her, watching as they put her in the back seat of a car. He wanted to get in and go with her, but someone, one of her friends, someone he had known his entire life, told him to stay. They assured him that she would be all right. He wanted to scream, so he did. He'd caused the rail to break and send her falling to the ground. He may have killed his own child.

"I should take you home," Blaine told him, his face somber.

Asher glanced back around to the house. The accident instigated the party's collapse. Streams of people emptied the abandoned building as the music faded and the lights inside dimmed, while a row of ruby taillights formed as cars exited down the rutted and overgrown lane and out onto the highway.

"C'mon," Blaine prodded him.

Had no one else seen his clumsiness causing the accident, and likely hurting Jessica and the baby? One moment she had stood there, looking out into the summer night, the next splayed on the ground in front of him, hurt and bleeding. Why didn't they accuse him? Why weren't they pursuing him as he dodged people and cars on his way back to the car?

Neither talked on the drive back to Asher's house, where the blue glare of the television lit the living room window. Had his mom not gone to the bar, or did she have some man over she'd met while out? Another loser she hoped would set her free?

"You okay?" Blaine asked once he brought the car to a stop. His face still reflecting a dark mood.

"I'll be fine," Asher answered in a tired voice. He climbed out of the car and slowly started across the yard as the Toyota's engine faded to silence. What would he say to her once he went inside? He could not bear to discuss the accident right now. There were too many uncertainties. What if the police arrived sometime in the night to arrest him for assault? But he had not assaulted her; he did not touch her, at least not before she fell. The rotted rail on the porch of an abandoned house had given way. Sure, his actions broke it, but not intentionally.

He stepped up onto the porch and paused again, still not ready to go inside. But despite his evasive inclination, he reached out and turned the knob, allowing the door to swing open. His mother looked up at him from her normal spot on the sofa. A glass of her vodka and orange juice sitting on the table in front of her.

"Hi, honey," she offered, a gentle smile on her face.

He offered a quiet "hello" in return and stepped inside. She sat alone, watching television—no night out at the bar, and no barfly brought home.

"Just watching some trash on TV," she explained, still smiling. "Didn't want to go out tonight."

How long had it been since she'd stayed home on a Saturday night instead of going out to the bar? He wanted to run off to his bedroom and cry, but here she was, not out at her dive bar, but trying to be part of the home. He sat down on the sofa beside her. An almost overbearing inner pain and uncertainty welled inside him; he would not leave her alone tonight. He would sit with her on their feeble old sofa, another hand-me-down from his dead great-grandmother, and watch some inane program. Tomorrow, when he knew more about Jessica's condition, he would try to tell her what happened.

CHAPTER THIRTEEN

NO TEXTS OR calls came from Jessica during the night and into the morning, though he did not expect her to reach out to him directly. Thus, as he spent the time unable to sleep and restraining himself from reaching out to her, a dark cloud of angst shrouded him. Finally, amidst his numbed motions of getting ready for work, one of her friends, one he had once also considered his friend, called. They shared with him the vibe in the car on the drive to Springfield, during which Jessica seemed more relieved than worried. Her mother arrived at the ER in theatrical hysterics, followed by the uncle, who silently lurked in the waiting room while leering at the gathered group of friends. They then shared her injuries, most notably a concussion, caused by her head hitting the ground, and a miscarriage.

"Miscarriage," Asher mumbled, then repeated the word to himself several times once off the phone. He'd caused it. His clumsiness and letting himself become so easily overwhelmed. Had he restrained himself and held back on his emotions the railing would not have broken and he would not have killed his own child. At least, he thought it his child despite Jessica's cryptic comment in the moment before the accident. After all, in a town the size of White Oak City, wouldn't he have heard if she was involved with someone else? He sent Blaine a message, letting him know what happened, but asked him not to call him until later.

He went to work stuck in a stupor, nearly oblivious to everything going on around him. The detached behavior seemed to please old Sam, but in Sally, it triggered concern, prompting her to ask him several times during his shift if he felt all right. He knew Sally soon would hear the tragic details from the town's gossips, as well as his own mother, so he saw no purpose in sharing it with her while it sat as an oppressive weight on his chest.

After work, he walked, or really ambled rather than walked, the few blocks home, despite Sally asking multiple times if she could take him there in her car. He could not bear questioning, as his thoughts still felt cloudy and unformed, leaving the reality of the last twenty-four hours framed in his mind like an episode of an old television show. Nearing his house, he saw the familiar hue of the reflection of the television in the front window. A sight so simplistic and ordinary, but one that began to clear his mind. Another night when his mother skipped the bar and stayed home.

He pushed the door open and found her seated in her favorite spot. She had her regular drink on the coffee table and some low-brow reality show on television. It needed to happen now. He needed to tell her about last night and Jessica, even if he knew it would make him cry. He sat on the sofa beside her, grabbed the remote, and turned off the TV. For a second, they stared at each other, him unsure of what to say, her eyes expecting something momentous. He took a deep breath, then shared the story of the night before and its tragic result. They both cried. He the most—tears flowing down his face as she held him and patted him, offering him well-meaning but cliché platitudes, the type that assumed everything happened as God intended. He did not doubt her sincerity in being upset, or her empathy at his distress, but he also sensed in her a relief, as if the events squelched some nightmare or lingering disappointment.

Three days passed before Jessica finally texted him. She said she felt much better and wanted to see him. He invited her to his house, but she said no, instead suggesting the steps of the old high school building.

As a child going to White Oak City's elementary school, a decidedly institutional building in the aesthetic of the late 1950s, Asher had looked forward to being a student in the majestic old high school building, a two story redbrick edifice with a bell tower jutting high in the middle and creating a symmetrical divide in the façade. But, by the time he filtered through the elementary and junior high buildings, the district had built a new high school and abandoned the old, leaving it a hulking relic bookending the eastern terminus of Commercial Street. Thus, he never spent a day of his adolescence in its long hallways, full of ancient lockers and doors with six-paned transom windows above them. Progress, so called, cheated him of the opportunity to experience his brooding teenage years in the same rooms his mother and grandmother had.

Instead, he worked his way to adulthood in the generic halls of a flat, unimaginative building. One that in a wealthier school district might have a few soaring atriums or advanced laboratories, but despite it being the only high school in Decatur County, it could not be more blandly utilitarian. They'd sacrificed the beauty of the old school without getting anything substantial in return.

Anxious about meeting up with Jessica, he left the house nearly ten minutes earlier than needed to make it to the old high school by eleven. He did it not to arrive early, but because he could not stop pacing back and forth between the living room and the kitchen. He needed to get out of the house. Though outside, in the boiling humidity of the day, his anxiety gave him a chill. He shook it off as best he could, stepping quickly down the porch steps and crossing the yard to the sidewalk.

The sun's heat reflected against him from the concrete of the sidewalk and the asphalt of the street. He imagined the sound of the rubber soles of his shoes sizzling each time they made contact with the ground. He glanced at his phone. At his current walking speed, he would be there fifteen minutes early, not just ten. He cut across the center of the park in the town square, passing the bandstand he'd leapt from to escape Tommy's attack. The chirping of thousands of cicadas serenaded him, the sharp clicking of their song scratching itself into his brain as the sun seared his skin. Reaching Commercial Street, he swung left. The old high school, glowing bright orange in the late morning sun, monopolized his view, and on its overgrown front steps sat Jessica, waiting for him.

She looked tired and frail, her eyes sunken and face pale. Even her expression sagged as she looked down the steps at him, her arms folded tight against her body, as if she were experiencing a chill in the miserable heat. He nodded as he climbed the steps, unsure how to greet her, and sat beside her without so much as nudging her. For a moment, they both quietly stared down the lifeless stretch of Commercial Street laid out in front of them.

"How are you feeling?" he finally asked, using his nervous right hand to fidget with his shoelace.

"Better," she quietly answered. "My headache is gone and—" She paused. "—my belly isn't hurting anymore."

Tears bubbled up in Asher's eyes. "It's my fault," he whimpered. "I'm so sorry."

She turned her face toward him, her eyes stern. "No, it wasn't," she told him. "My fall was an accident. You didn't do anything wrong. You've never done anything wrong."

He shook his head and a couple of tears dropped down onto the step where his feet rested, evaporating as they hit. "I could have done more to take care of you and the baby," he cried out.

Her arm slipped around his waist, and she pulled him close, laying her head on his shoulder.

"Do you know why I said yes to you when you asked me to prom?" she asked him.

He shook his head.

"You've always acted nice to me and never wanted anything from me," she explained. "I've known you forever. You were my friend. We shouldn't have drunk alcohol or had sex that night. You didn't really want to, but I wanted to be in charge, and you wanted to make me happy."

Her description of the night made him feel exposed and uncomfortable. "Sure, I wanted to," he protested though he knew it a lie. He wanted to go home, or work, or somewhere else. Talking about the baby and accident did not bother him, but this caused his body to grow tense.

A kind smile appeared on her face. "You wanted to because every boy wants to, at least to a degree, but you didn't really want to with me," she countered. "You did because I pushed for it, and you don't like to let people down. Then we did. And it did make me feel in control, that it was up to me. That's why I kept coming to your house—because it was up to me. You weren't telling me when.

Or forcing me. I did that. Most of the time you watched TV when we did it."

Asher's hands shook. It had always been her idea. But he followed along because he felt a responsibility, not a desire, and he wanted to make his friend happy.

"I felt safe with you," she continued, still leaning against him. "I didn't love you, even though you are good-looking, especially now, with your face shaved and your stylish new haircut. I guess you finally figured out you're hot." She let out a quiet laugh.

"I would have married you for the baby," he offered.

"I know," she told him. "If you had been some normal boyfriend, and I got pregnant by you, maybe I would have even if you didn't love me."

A new feeling of ease began to bloom in Asher's chest, but he sensed she had more to tell him.

"I would have taken care of the baby," he explained. "I'm not my father."

She shook her head. "I don't think it was your baby," she admitted.

A spike of anger and jealousy made his body flush and go rigid. But instead of lashing out and saying something cruel, he took a deep breath and settled back. "Whose baby was it?" he asked, his voice terse despite trying to repress his ire.

A sob escaped her. "It's horrible," she cried out.

The tone inclined to a dark truth.

"You can tell me," he told her, his arm now around her, holding her up. "I won't tell anyone."

She nodded. "I know you won't," she answered in a cracking voice. "It's horrible, and I've not told anyone. My mom—she must know, but she hasn't done anything. It's not even the first baby. I think I was pregnant last summer too. One morning my stomach hurt, and I went to the bathroom and a bunch of blood and little lumps of blood came out. I didn't tell anyone. I didn't want anyone to know." Her body heaved as choking sobs escaped her while tears poured from her eyes.

"Your uncle," he whispered, finally understanding. "Your goddamn uncle."

No words, only a slight nod in response.

He wrapped his arms tighter around her, pulling her as close to him as he could. Most days he thought of only his own difficulties—being poor, his mother's unraveling life, and the continuing abuse from Tommy Summer—but Jessica suffered in a way that was much worse. His chest ached as he imagined life in her house, the constant tension only broken when away from home. How did he miss it? How had he been so oblivious to the torment she lived? In school, they talked about warning signs for suicide and other issues among peers, but how could teenagers, all embroiled in the trauma of adolescence, be empathetic enough to notice?

"I'm so sorry," he told her. Her body shivered in his arms, the force of each sob nearly breaking loose his hold. "I would have tried to help if I'd known. I thought you were mad at me because I got you pregnant, but it wasn't my baby."

Jessica gently pulled herself out of his embrace. "I don't know for certain it wasn't, but I knew it could have been his, and it felt like it was his—to me," she explained, her eyes red from weeping.

Maybe he had been a father, at least briefly. Maybe his child did die. Maybe she could have done more to protect it. The thoughts crowded his head, but they disturbed him, made him feel selfish, so he pushed them back out. How horrible, to go nine months carrying a baby and not knowing who the father was—the boyfriend or the uncle who'd raped her—a circumstance void of the happiness that should be automatic when a baby was expected. It was also an immoral ugliness, perpetrated by someone who knew better and should have protected her, not abused her.

"Are you going to go to the police?" he asked.

For a moment, she did not respond, only gazed across the street in the direction of the old church that sat on the corner, its massive double doors and steeple glaring back, as if delivering judgment. "I wasn't," she finally answered. "I figured he would leave me alone now. But, last night, I was in my room and he came in and stood there staring at me. My mom walked by and looked in, but didn't say anything. She just stood there for a moment until he left the room. Why didn't she say something? She knows but won't do anything."

The tears had abated, with only sniffles escaping her now, as if she reconciled her mother's apathy as accepted behavior.

"Do you want me to come with you to the police?" he asked.

She shook her head. "Mrs. Donovan is going with me," she answered.

"She's helping me to go to college," Asher replied.

Jessica smiled. "You're going to have an amazing life," she told him.

Inside, he felt optimism, despite the ugliness of what he'd just learned. "You too," he offered. "We both just have to work for it."

CHAPTER FOURTEEN

IN HIS TWO months working in the restaurant industry, Asher came to fully appreciate one of its universal truths—Friday night brought in the money. Even on a rainy one, though only one Friday evening all summer saw any significant precipitation, customers poured inside. It typically started around five thirty and did not stop until Sally quit seating tables around nine fifteen. Though the restaurant closed at nine, she reasoned some folks got delayed, and no one liked a hardnose.

On these days, old Sam turned authoritarian about procedure, demanding every plate, utensil, and glass go through the dishwasher prior to five, when the older patrons began to trickle in to eat. From there, Asher worked at his top speed the entire evening, clearing tables and keeping the dirty dishes moving through the dishwashing process. He occasionally helped wait on tables in those rare times when the ever-resourceful and efficient Sally got behind, usually with every table full for a three-hour block. But despite the routine craziness of Friday nights, Asher never complained, as Sally always gave him a hefty lump of cash at the end of the night—his share of the tips.

"Busier than usual, tonight, even for a Friday," Sally remarked as she dropped a bin of dirty dishes on the counter by the dishwasher.

Asher glanced back to the clock on the wall. It showed 10:27 p.m.

"And later than normal getting out," he replied. Usually, he'd be on his way home by ten twenty on a Friday.

"Hot days make people hungry," she commented. "Your house doesn't have air-conditioning, does it?"

He shook his head, wishing he could say otherwise. "It's miserable, but Mom says it'd make the electric bill too expensive," he told her.

"She's right," she responded. "And plenty of people have lived without it their entire lives."

He shrugged his shoulders in an apathetic agreement.

"Tomorrow's your birthday, right?" she asked.

He smiled in response, feeling excited for turning eighteen, despite having no plans to celebrate.

"What are you doing for it?"

"Same as every Saturday. Come here," he said with a smile.

A scoff escaped her.

"You are not," she argued.

He shrugged his shoulders. He had no plans, and no else made any for him, nor did he expect them to, so why not work and earn money?

"I talked to your cousin, the one in Springfield, earlier. She told me it was your birthday and asked me if you could get off work early. Guess what I told her?"

Asher stopped loading dishes onto the dish rack and turned to face Sally. "What?" he asked.

"You have the whole day off and are getting paid for it," she explained with a huge smile.

"Wait! What?" he cried out, his face breaking out into a broad, goofy grin.

"You need to have fun on your birthday," she instructed him.

Of everyone in his life, outside of his grandmother, Sally did more than most to encourage him—even more than Mrs. Donovan. She'd hired him, she listened to him and got nothing from it, at least nothing he yet understood. And everything she did for him, she did with gentle eyes and a warm smile. Why did what happened to him matter to her?

"You don't need to do that," he replied. "But thank you. I guess that's why Raina asked me what time I'm waking up in the morning."

Sally nodded. "Almost done with the dishes?" she asked.

"Five more minutes," he happily answered, his entire body feeling energized despite the last ten hours of work.

"Hurry up, and you can walk me home," she told him.

Despite the sun having sunk deep below the horizon, a hot and sticky humidity stubbornly clung to the air when Asher and Sally stepped outside the diner's front door. He paused for a moment, peering into the darkness of the park across the street, while she locked the door behind him. Since the attack, in the evening's darkness, the park and its weathered old bandstand had given him an almost sinister chill. Sally stepped beside him and gave a quick glance in the same direction and then, without saying a word, took hold of his arm and led him toward the courthouse. She lived a few blocks east of the square, up on the town's most prominent hill that a century earlier held reign as the most fashionable neighborhood in White Oak City.

"How've you been?" she asked as they passed in front of the courthouse, its massive four columns supporting an eave-set clock, one with hands frozen in time longer than he had lived.

"Okay, I guess," he answered.

"I heard about Jessica, and the baby," she said, her voice void of either emotion or judgment. "I didn't know until tonight. I usually hear gossip much sooner than that."

A sigh escaped him.

"We don't have to talk about it," she said.

"It's okay," he replied. "It's probably better, how it all turned out."

Sally put her arm around him and pulled him close as they walked up the hill. "Who knows what's better, but it's the way it is, so we move forward," she responded.

"There's more to the story, but I can't tell you yet," he said. "It'll all come out soon, though, because I don't think they'll be able to keep it quiet."

She slowed her pace, and he slowed in turn. "It has something to do with her uncle, doesn't it?" she asked.

"How do you know?" Asher replied, halting in his surprise and bringing them to a complete stop.

"I heard he was arrested today," she explained. "He was always creepy. A couple years ahead of me in school, but he paid too much attention to younger girls. It was...unsettling."

A couple tears trickled down Asher's cheeks. "Why didn't someone do something sooner?" he asked. "He'd been doing it to her for years. She said her mom must have known, but did nothing."

Sally shook her head. "Fear—maybe her mom was afraid, and sometimes it's easier to ignore the truth," she said. "There are dozens of reasons why she might not have said something, all psychological and based on her own fear or experience. Maybe he abused her too. Maybe it was money, maybe their church, maybe how they would be looked at or judged if it came out."

Unease roiled his stomach, the thought of years of abuse making him feel sick. The injustice. The fact that trivial concerns, such as how it would look to others, or money, or something else, may have left Jessica there in that household. How did people live with themselves after doing such horrible things? How did her mother live with herself?

"Why are people so horrible?" he asked, not expecting an answer but feeling a need to say it out loud.

"Not everyone is," she responded. "You're not. You're a very nice young man. Don't let the ugly people discourage you. There are a lot of good people here in this town. Sometimes they just get hidden by the actions of the bad ones."

Good people, right here in White Oak City? He could name a few who treated him well and not only Sally or his grandmother, the obvious ones. But it did seem harder to search them out in his own thoughts as the ugly ones came quicker to mind. Maybe the modesty of the good ones obscured them in his memory. *Why did unpleasant memories seem so much more powerful and permanent, and good ones fleeting, only to occasionally appear and vanish with a scent or a sound?*

"What other gossip do you know?" Asher asked as they started walking again. He needed a shift in the conversation, something to calm his unease.

"Lots," she answered. "We know who your daddy is, as bad as

he may be, but I know of at least two people in this town who think they know who their daddies are, but they would be wrong," she offered with a smile.

"Who?" Asher excitedly asked, curious to know who else held a scandalous pedigree.

Sally shook her head. "Not my gossip to tell, only hint at," she replied.

He grunted in response.

"I do have a story about your late grandfather, but only if you promise not to mention it to your grandmother," she said.

"What about my mom?" he asked.

"She's already heard it," Sally clarified. "They say he once killed a man out in California in the 1930s, when he was young."

Again, Asher stopped walking, picturing the calm and quiet man he remembered, but as a killer. "That's crazy," he replied, not sure if he should believe it.

"Did you know he had a wife and kid before he met your grandmother, and they died during the Great Depression?" she asked.

Asher nodded. This story he had heard. His grandfather's younger life. Before he moved to Missouri and married a second time, to a woman nearly twenty years younger.

"Evidently, while he lived and worked on some farm in California, the first wife got sick. But the boss who owned the farm wouldn't call the doctor, so she died," Sally explained.

Most of the story he knew, though without the part of the boss not calling the doctor, as his grandmother told him the rest years earlier, shortly after his grandfather died. "I knew most of that," he responded.

"But, do you know that after that he went crazy and beat the boss to death?" she asked.

"No," he exclaimed, and followed it with a gasp.

"That's the story," she replied, then shrugged her shoulders. "I've never heard about anything that proves it, though, just the rumor. And I didn't hear it until your grandfather had died, so I don't know if anyone asked him about it. They say Alvin Brock wasn't his real name, just one he assumed so he could hide from the law."

Could it possibly be true? His kind, giving grandfather murdered someone? It seemed impossible, although he only knew his grandfather as an old man, nearly eighty by the time of Asher's birth. Maybe some clue to it existed on the internet—a mystery to solve. But why did he need a mystery to solve? He had enough to solve in his daily life, mainly figuring out how to pay for college.

"Does my mom believe it?" he asked.

Sally shook her head. "She doesn't believe anything bad about her daddy," she answered. "He was almost sixty when she was born, so she never knew him as young. Maybe he calmed down as he got older. I've never heard anyone say anything bad about his life here. Just the one story about before he came to White Oak City."

They reached the top of the hill, with the house Sally shared with her new husband and father down the street on the right, across from an old yellow mansion that housed the funeral home. Asher could not imagine how Sally and her husband stood to live with old Sam, unless he acted less grouchy at home. Or maybe they all knew how to keep out of each other's way. They had a big Victorian house, after all, not as large as the neighboring mortuary but enough so as to give them space to avoid each other. Unlike the two-bedroom hovel he and his mother shared.

"When is your cousin coming to get you tomorrow?" Sally asked.

He pulled his phone out of his pocket and skimmed through his text messages. "She says be dressed and ready by 10:30 a.m.," he replied.

"Have fun tomorrow, and happy birthday an hour early," Sally said before kissing him on the cheek.

CHAPTER FIFTEEN

"TRY THIS ON," Raina demanded as she shoved a red button-down shirt into Asher's hands.

"Where?" he asked her, glancing around the thrift shop for some privacy.

"Here," she demanded.

"Don't they have a little room where I can do that?" he whined, his voice getting higher with each word.

"This isn't Saks," she answered with a laugh.

He looked around again. Dozens of shoppers thronged the thrift store, browsing aisle by aisle, though the men's section felt slightly less crowded than the women's area. He unbuttoned the red shirt and started to put it on over the button-down he already had on.

"What are you doing?" Raina cried out. "Take that one off first. You can't wear one over the other. This isn't the eighties."

His face heated up with embarrassment. "I'm not wearing a T-shirt under it," he replied.

"So?" she responded, flipping her hands up in exasperation.

With a hard swallow to stifle his shyness, he unbuttoned his shirt and pulled it off.

"Oh my god," Raina loudly called out, an amused look on her face.

"Wh-what?" Asher cried, nervously looking around.

"I think that old lady over there is getting hot from looking at your rocking body," she replied, followed by a loud laugh, which garnered several looks from across the store.

"Stop that," he warned in a hushed voice as he hurriedly pulled the red shirt on, feeling his entire body sweating from the embarrassment, despite the store's cool temperature.

"It's a joke, little cousin," she said with a smile. "You do have a nice body. The girls must be lining up, especially with that new haircut and smooth face. Thank God for that. You were beginning to look a little feral."

A nervous laugh escaped him. He glanced around again, spotting a mirror hanging on a column a few feet away. "I think this is too small," he commented as he stepped toward the mirror, but after seeing his reflection, he realized that while the shirt fit tight, it did so in the right places and made his arms and chest look muscular and well formed.

"If you don't get laid tonight, I'll lose all faith in teenage girls," she offered. "When did you go from being my sweet, although a bit dorky, cousin to full-on stud? And red is your color. No doubt about that."

Even slight praise made him feel uneasy as he never knew how to reply. And his cousin's over-the-top response exceeded anything subtle, causing his body to tense and his hands to tremor slightly. But despite this unconfident reaction, he could not help but feel handsome when looking into the mirror. How could someone with such a mess of a family, who constantly worried about how his life would turn out, look so good? Maybe he should try modeling or acting? No, he knew better than that. The thought of people staring at him and judging him for his looks would send him into some dark seclusion. Some people thrived on that type of attention. Not him. Sure, he enjoyed getting some appreciation, but not being paraded around like a prize cow.

"I think I want to get the shirt," he mumbled shyly.

"Yeah, you do," she responded followed by another laugh. "Now, you need a pair of clubbing jeans."

"Clubbing?" he asked.

"Yes, clubbing," she replied. "Today is your eighteenth birthday, so I'm taking you to a club that you can go to when you're eighteen. You can't drink, because they put a big black X on each of your hands, but we'll do some dancing and hang out with some of my friends."

The confidence built from seeing himself in the shirt instantly eroded. "I can't dance," he said in protest.

Raina offered him a smile that held a hint of condescension. "It doesn't matter," she assured him. "There will be so many people dancing, we'll just kind of join in with the group. No one is looking at anyone, even with you sporting the guns in that red shirt."

The idea of dancing at a club felt overwhelming. But didn't turning eighteen deserve something special? And Raina wanted to make sure he remembered it.

"Is R.J. coming?" he asked.

"You mean my country-as-a-tractor brother?" she responded while handing him a pair of jeans.

"Yeah," he answered. He unfolded the jeans and looked them up and down, unsure of what else to do with them.

"No, absolutely not," she protested. "I love my brother, but we will not be going to his type of place."

Asher smiled thinking about his hulking cousin on a dance floor trying to move to the pounding pulse of hip-hop. "What do I do with these?" he asked, holding the jeans up between them.

"Try them on," she replied.

"What?" he gasped. "I can't do that here; there are people everywhere."

She gave a quick glance around the store, then pulled him

back into an aisle of men's suits. "There's no one back here," she told him. "I'll block this end. Just be quick about going from your shorts to the jeans."

Why couldn't they have gone to a store with changing rooms? He looked around, thinking maybe he could change quickly enough and not get caught in his underwear like some pervert.

"Hurry," Raina urged him.

He unbuttoned his shorts and let them drop to the floor, then stuck a leg into the pants. They felt like rubber bands stretched around his legs. He would never be able to pull them all the way up. "They're too tight," he called out.

Raina turned around to see. "What are you wearing?" she cried out.

Asher froze. What did she mean? At the other end of the aisle, a middle-aged woman stopped and stared at him for a moment, then shook her head and walked on to the next aisle. "You gave them to me," he whined.

"Not those, your white, or should I say yellow, underwear that's full of holes," she exclaimed.

Looking down, he had to agree, though most of his briefs at home looked similar. "It's all I have," he admitted.

Raina shook her head. "Fine, finish trying on the jeans, then we'll go somewhere to get you underwear, because you're not getting laid in those," she replied.

"I don't want to get laid," he barked back, getting another

round of stares from other shoppers in response to the remark. A moment of embarrassment that gave him the jolt he needed to pull the jeans the rest of the way on, and despite his legs feeling as if they were wrapped in plastic wrap, he also got a nod of approval from his cousin.

"Then don't get laid," she said. "But we're still getting you underwear, and not from here. I don't want to be responsible for you getting crabs."

Used underwear did seem unsanitary to him. "What are crabs?" he asked.

A loud laugh escaped her. "You are too cute," she replied. "Put your shorts back on, and let's go get you some undies."

The embarrassment of their time together in the thrift shop only continued once they reached the underwear section at the discount store across the parking lot. Just nearing the boxes full of colorful jockey shorts made him nervous, as dozens of other shoppers grazed in the same area. The much sparser crowd at the secondhand store suddenly made used underwear seem preferable.

"You're not going to make me try these on, are you?" he asked in a whisper.

A gush of laughter poured out of her. "Yes, strip naked here in the aisle and try a pair on," she joked.

A warm flush filled his face and crawled down his back. "I don't know," he whimpered. "I never go clothes shopping."

A loud sigh escaped her. "Sorry, Ash. I know, and that's why we're here," she offered. She then slid her arm around his shoulder and led him between the rows of underwear, a selection of more colors and designs than he realized existed. The only ones his mother ever purchased for him came in plain white with a high waist.

Raina's fingers quickly danced across the boxes of underwear, pulling off five or six as she went along, and handing them to him in turn. He gave each a quick look as it landed in his hands. They all held between three to five pairs in a variety of colors and patterns, none white.

"Briefs—you have to get briefs—there is nothing sexy about boxers," she instructed him. "My dad wears boxers. R.J. wears boxers. No one sexy wears them. And you should have some that are fun." She held one of the boxes up in front of him. "These have wild animals on them—here are lions, zebras, and elephants," she explained. "You need at least a couple pair. What do you think of bikini cut?"

The picture on the box she now held up showed a muscular man wearing a tiny pair of underwear that seemed to provide only minimal coverage. The thought of putting those on, even in the privacy of his bedroom, made him blush. It did not help that the aisle seemed a lot more popular now, with a mass of hands sifting through the racks of underwear and T-shirts, all while his cousin continued to push boxes featuring nearly naked men into his face.

"I don't want those," he nervously insisted, while grabbing a box that came in a variety of colors but offered more modesty. "These—these are good."

Raina shrugged in response. "Baby steps," she declared, after which she thrust the box of underwear with exotic animals on them into his free hand. "These too," she insisted.

Next, she led him a couple aisles away to a shelf cluttered with dozens of bottles of cologne.

"This is your birthday present from my mom and dad," she explained. "Well, Mom really. She told me to get you some cologne since you're a man now."

His face turned red. A man in age, he thought to himself, but in many ways, he still felt like a boy.

She grabbed hold of his wrist and turned it over, holding it for a moment as she spritzed cologne on it. "Give it a second to air out, then take a whiff," she instructed him.

He counted down from ten in his head, then brought his wrist up to his nose and sniffed. It reminded him of the rotten mustiness of the bathroom in his house, causing his nose to crinkle up in disgust.

"Not that one, then," she surmised after watching his expression. She grabbed his other wrist and gave it a spray. He counted down again and raised it for a quick sniff.

It soothed him, clean and light—how he imagined the ocean smelled, despite never having visited the ocean. "That one," he said.

"That's a start. Here, let's try a few others," she offered.

He shook his head. "No, this one is good," he replied, taking a step back from her as he did so.

"You don't want to compare some of the others?" she asked, pointing to the dozens of options.

He shook his head again, overwhelmed by the day's shopping trip and ready to stop. The idea of shopping itself did not bother him, as he enjoyed getting new clothes and being able to smell good. Instead, his own nervousness and feeling of ineptness in the process itself drained the pleasure he knew he should feel. After all, he could count on his fingers the number of times in his life he'd gone shopping for clothes.

Most of his clothing up to now came in boxes or bags of freebies someone would give his mom. The only new stuff he got came on his birthday or at Christmas, when his grandmother would buy him clothes, always plain rather than stylish but at least new, not the universally used stuff his mom provided.

Maybe this would become his new reality, something he could get used to, buying clothes for himself that looked good on him and had not been passed down from someone else. This must be how most people got their clothes anyway, not scavenged from a mismatched collection bundled in black trash bags, with half of it being old or torn and the other half the wrong size. A life that did not depend on walking around in someone else's throwaways, or, even when so, it could be at least something he picked out himself in the type of shop where Raina took him. Of course, he would still prefer going to a store with the convenience of a changing room.

CHAPTER SIXTEEN

NOT ONE FAMILIAR face, except that of his cousin Raina, sat around the restaurant table, despite it being his birthday. He wanted to invite Blaine, but he had another three months of being seventeen, so his cousin said no. Any other of his friends had the same problem, as he was one of the oldest in his class. The result of being held back in the first grade, an action justified with the reasoning of him not being as mature as the other students. That lack of maturity at an early stage in his formal education must have had little or no tie to intelligence as he already carried the title of presumptive valedictorian, at least among his teachers. His delayed progression in school should have helped shield him from his childhood antagonist, Tommy Summer, who was born two weeks before him. But

Tommy was also held back in the third grade, ensuring the conflict to come.

Regardless of being surrounded by a group of strangers in celebration of his entrance into adulthood, Asher found it easy to relax, at least after the initial rush of greetings. For those first few moments threatened to overwhelm him as new acquaintances hugged him and offered an embarrassing amount of birthday wishes. They even presented a card with money in it. Upon receiving it, his face flushed red with embarrassment and his eyes watered nearly to tears because of their thoughtfulness. He probably would have demanded his cousin take him home right then if not for the confidence he felt wearing his new clothes, having had Raina fix his hair, and knowing he smelled good thanks to the cologne. Luckily, that rush of initial greetings quickly calmed, and his trepidation waned.

Sitting around the large restaurant table, his cousin, in the chair on his right side, kept the conversation flowing. He appreciated her act of charity, and he noticed whenever he glanced around the table, Raina's friends always smiled if they caught his eye—every one of them. They were a party of eight: himself and four girls and three boys, or four women and three men, all at least a couple years older than his new eighteen. In fact, he suspected all had passed the iconic age of twenty-one, based on the beer and wine they all enjoyed, while a soda sat on the table in front of him. Raina seemed the alpha among them, all of whom she knew from college. She'd chosen the restaurant, a chain Italian place known for its endless pasta, and mapped out the night, including who rode in whose car, all based on expected alcohol intake. As an adult out in the world, she retained a personality true to her childhood origins, a time when she had no problem dictating what games to play or adventures to have. And who else could have corralled her adult friends into helping babysit an eighteen-year-old cousin on his birthday?

"Are you having a good birthday so far?" a man asked him.

Asher looked across the table at him. Raina had introduced him as Larry when they first met outside the restaurant, and now they faced each other.

"I am," Asher answered, a shy smile on his face. "Raina took me shopping earlier. It was kind of embarrassing."

Larry smiled. He had a big smile that made his already striking blue eyes seem brighter. "Why's that?" he asked.

"She made me try on the clothes in the aisle at the store," he replied while shaking his head.

Larry's head tilted to the side as he thought about the comment. "Wait—strip down, then try them on out in the open?" he queried.

Asher nodded.

A laugh escaped Larry, but not one that felt demeaning to Asher—instead, a soft "Hee-hee-hee," which seemed more of an appreciated acknowledgment of the younger man's embarrassment.

"Then she was very insistent on the type of underwear I got,"

Asher added.

Larry's smile grew big again. His face seemed almost plain when unamused, but distractingly handsome when happiness shone through. "Raina, did you really tell him what type of underwear to get?" he asked her.

"I'm simply putting the boy on the right path in life," she responded, her nose darting up in the air in a pretentious manner. "Now, anyone who sees him in his underwear will know they made a good decision."

The table broke out into laughter, but none of it felt condescending to Asher, instead, supportive. He could not imagine his friends from school reacting the same way. They would make crass comments or give belittling looks.

Not once at dinner did he feel like an outsider. His cousin's friends acted genuinely interested in talking with him and making him one of their group, without singling him out by trying too hard. He tried to return the hospitality, though he could tell his attention returned to Larry an inordinate amount of the time. His face exuded warmth in its smile, and in his comments and questions, his personality within bubbled as well, one with good-natured wit and a genuine interest in his friends' lives.

"Are you ready to go dancing?" Larry asked as the group went through the process of paying their checks, except for Asher, who got another birthday gift in the form of those at the table splitting his.

"I'm not good at dancing," Asher responded, anxiety tingling in his gut at the thought of being on a dance floor in the middle of a bunch of strangers. But imagining being on a dance floor in front of people he knew seemed more daunting.

"No worries, I'll show you some moves," Larry offered, a smile lighting up his face more than before.

"Larry," Raina cried out, startling Asher with her volume. "Stop flirting with him."

Larry's face reddened. "I'm not flirting, just saying I can show him some moves," he offered in protest, his smile slipping from exuberant to shy in the process.

Asher offered a timid smile in response. He had started to suspect Larry might be gay, but his cousin's comment seemed to confirm it. He knew a girl at school who identified as a lesbian, and Mrs. Donovan's son got beaten up by a group of boys from school a few years earlier for being gay. But other than those two, he could not think of a single other person he knew who had come out. Until now, as now he knew Larry. Suddenly, he felt extremely glad that Blaine wasn't allowed to come out with them.

The next stop of the night came in a run-down part of the city, an old redbrick warehouse turned nightclub nestled among the old mills on Phelps Street. A cavernous space on the inside, two stories high with massive multipaned windows dominating the upper half of the walls. But whatever goods it once stored and distributed no longer mattered, as it now housed dozens of young adults, dancing to pop and house music with little care for their lives outside its walls. The place was designed as an escape, though for Asher's painfully self-aware personality, the more of an escape a place appeared, the less likely he could. He found it overwhelming and in contrast to how he typically relaxed and enjoyed himself but did not want to disappoint his cousin, who had planned it with him in mind. Maybe if he let his guard down a little, he could have a good time.

Their group of eight cut across the dance floor on their way to the bar, which at ten p.m., early by club standards, had yet to get bogged down with a mass of drunken partiers. One of Raina's friends ordered eight beers, but the bartender knew better than to line them up, first asking to see the hands of everyone who would get one. A shudder of concern ran through the group, as Asher wore a large black *X* on the back of each of his hands.

"Just six actually. Asher and I are driving so only drinking soda," Larry offered, helping cool the tension and keeping them from getting kicked out before they even started dancing.

The six who would get a beer then raised their hands as proof of age. The bartender grunted in acknowledgement and offered a warning. "If I find any of you giving alcohol to a minor, all of you will be out." The group replied with a synchronized and quiet nod, then grabbed their drinks and crossed back to the opposite side of the dance floor, safely out of the bartender's view.

"Sorry about that, Ash," Raina said once they settled into a space on the edge of the growing throng of dancers. "We'll get you a beer in a bit when it's busier and we aren't worried about being watched."

Asher shook his head. "I'm good with soda," he assured her.

She smiled at him. "Are you sure? It is your birthday."

"I'm good," he replied.

They chatted among themselves for around half an hour, then a new and trendy song began to play, so Raina grabbed hold of Asher's hand. She pulled him out onto the dance floor, the rest of the group following along. He took a deep breath and tried moving to the music but felt rigid and awkward. How did something that embarrassed him so much turn into the main event of his eighteenth birthday? He tried swaying back and forth, doing the bare minimum for standing in the middle of the dance floor. Around him, Raina and her friends jerked and shimmied along to the pulsing beat of the music. No one did the same thing, all twisting and turning at random. It helped ease his nerves to see so many others looking as awkward and stiff as he felt. The only difference being they at least tried to have a good time as they did it. People were so relaxed with themselves that they could move without worrying about what others might think of them and just embraced the music, feeling alive.

A hand gently patted Asher's shoulder. He glanced over to see Larry's grin.

"You're moving just fine," Larry assured him, then turned away as if shy about his forward remark.

"Thanks," Asher yelled back, trying to make sure Larry could hear him over the blasting music.

Larry nodded and grinned again. He then moved over to one of the girls in the group and started dancing with her, though every time Asher looked in their direction, he caught Larry looking back at him.

By eleven thirty, sweat streamed down Asher's forehead, soaking his eyebrows and funneling down to the tip of his nose, from where it dripped onto the floor. "I think I need a break before I collapse," he yelled into Raina's ear. The music had grown increasingly louder since they first arrived.

"Me too," she agreed, and followed him through the crowd of dancers to the edge of the room.

"Wow, we've been out there forty-five minutes," Asher said as he looked at the time on his phone. And, he realized, he'd had fun.

"It happens," Raina offered with a laugh.

He leaned back against the wall. His clothes felt soaked with sweat, again making him feel self-conscious, but glancing around, he noticed plenty of others looking the same way. He also noticed several girls watching him with smiles and interest. *I'm imagining it*, he told himself, so he looked around again, a little slower this time. They still watched him, giving him smiles from coy to almost obscene, one mouthing "hi" to him. He spotted one of the guys giving him a look that came across as more than casual, despite the guy having a girl pawing at him and trying to kiss him.

"Some of these girls are staring at me," Asher commented to his cousin, leaving out the guy doing the same thing.

"It wouldn't surprise me," Raina replied. "You are a total stud in those clothes. Take your pick if you want one," she offered with a laugh.

It made him uneasy when they leered at him. Not that he did not want to look attractive, but that they seemed to be dissecting him with their eyes. This was what women complained about—men ogling them with no subtlety to their interest. No wonder it pissed them off, but maybe a double standard sometimes existed. He noticed one woman staring at him for at least three minutes without looking away.

"Finding your mark?" Larry asked as he joined them, two fresh sodas in his hand. "This one's for you," he told Asher while handing him the cup in his right hand.

"Thank you. I need it," Asher replied, relieved by both the drink and the company.

Larry took a moment to look around them. "These girls are after you like they are in heat," he said with a laugh.

"You see it too?" Asher questioned.

"Oh, yeah," Larry replied. "But you're the one coming out here with your model looks and wearing a shirt that shows off your buff bod."

Asher felt his face go warm with embarrassment. He got embarrassed far too easily. "There's a guy over there who keeps looking at me," he said.

"Oh, which one?" Larry excitedly asked.

Trying not to appear obvious, Asher gave a subtle nod to the guy with the girl.

"He's not even cute," Larry replied with a laugh.

"And he's got a girlfriend or something," Asher added.

"A lot of them do," Larry responded, a sour look replacing his charming smile. "I've had so many married or closeted guys hit on me, it's ridiculous. I feel sorry for their wives and girlfriends."

Asher nodded. "I guess it is unfair to them, isn't it?" he agreed.

The smile reemerged on Larry's face. "We don't need to talk about this," he told Asher. "You see a girl here you want to say hi to? Maybe get her phone number?"

The question triggered a sudden shift inside Asher—he felt enlightened, like muddy creek water settling so one can see the gravel in the creek bed again. Much of his life had been muddy, a life filled with uncertainties caused by his mother, even developing his own sense of ethics seemed fuzzy rather than clear. Being poor probably impacted that. Poverty often meant trying to get something for free or paying little for it. Its desperation could lead to searching for false happiness in alcohol or drugs, a trajectory common around White Oak City. Sure, these problems existed among all economic classes, but they felt more bottomless for the poor. And right now, in a club full of partying and probably more than a little debauchery, he found a burst of clarity.

"I don't want to talk to any girl," Asher replied, his voice steady despite a growing nervousness in his stomach. "I want to talk to you."

Larry smiled though the tilt of his head hinted at confusion in his thoughts.

As it neared twelve thirty, the group dispersed into the night, the last holdouts of the birthday adventure arriving on Raina's front porch fifteen minutes later. Only five of the eight remained: Asher, Raina, her two roommates, and Larry, who had driven them all there. The evening's buzz wearing off, they quietly chatted and laughed among themselves in the warm night air as a small swarm of bugs crowded around the yellow glow of the porch light.

"Asher, you are now eighteen years and one day and have yet to have a birthday beer," Raina stated firmly as she pushed the front door open.

"I'm fine. I don't need one," he offered in protest.

"One. I insist you have at least one." She countered. "How about you Larry?"

Larry nodded. "I'll have one," he told her.

"Okay, inside," Raina instructed, with the two roommates obediently following.

But Asher shook his head. He enjoyed sitting out on a porch on a summer night. Of course he lived in a house with no air-conditioning, so it may have evolved as a habit of necessity. But regardless of its origin, he wanted to sit outside tonight, despite feeling the comforting cooling blast of the air conditioner through the open front door. "I'd rather sit here, but can you turn off the light so the bugs go away," he told her.

"How about you, Larry?" Raina asked.

Larry shook his head. "I'll stay here with Asher, if that's okay with him."

With a broad smile, Asher agreed.

"'K, I'm going to change really quick, but I'll be back with a couple beers soon," she told them.

The light clicked off, and after a moment, the buzzing and fluttering of the bugs began to fade. Asher dropped into a plastic lawn chair, while Larry leaned against the porch rail, with about four feet between them. Neither said anything for a few moments, just quietly listening until only the chirping cicadas could be heard.

"I hope you don't mind," Larry started, and then he paused. "Raina told me about your girlfriend and the baby. I'm sorry about it."

Even outside of White Oak City, his private life found eager ears. But no, he did not hear a gossipy vibe in Larry's tone. The man with the handsome smile who stood in the shadows in front of him intended no malice or personal enjoyment in mentioning it.

"I appreciate that," Asher responded as tears began to gather in his eyes.

"Can I ask a really personal question?" Larry quietly inquired.

"Sure," Asher answered.

"Did you want to be a dad?" he asked.

Nobody had ever asked him that question. Dozens of other questions got asked: What did he plan to do about college? How could he afford to take care of the child? But no one had asked him if he wanted it. He paused for a moment, thinking about it, about what he might have really wanted. "I don't know," he finally replied. "If it had been born, I'd want to be there for it—not hiding away like my father did."

Larry nodded. "My dad was around, but he's never really wanted to know me," he explained. "My personal life is ignored."

A burst of laughter came from inside the house—three young women having a good time.

"I'll never have to worry about getting a girl pregnant," Larry offered with a laugh.

Asher felt a wide smile spread across his own face. "I won't ever either again," he replied.

A quiet chuckle came from Larry. "You might feel that way now, but this will pass, and some other girl will catch your eye."

Asher shook his head. "No, and I know that for a fact," he replied in a serious voice.

"But..." Larry started, then stopped as Asher stood and walked toward him.

Despite the dark, Larry's eyes shone as Asher neared him. Only six inches separated their faces when he finally came to a stop. Tears, not of pain or fear, but emanating from a deep warmth within his chest, fogged Asher's eyes. Neither spoke, only gazed at each other, and then Asher tilted his head slightly to the right and leaned forward, his lips gently pressing against Larry's. The moment of contact enveloped Asher in an almost euphoric feeling, as if nothing else in his life would ever seem as right. They kissed only for a few seconds, and upon its release, Larry wrapped his arms tightly around Asher and held him close.

"I hoped that was going to happen," Larry quietly murmured as he held him.

"Really?" Asher whispered in response.

"Yeah, but right now I just want to hold you," he replied.

They stood in each other's embrace for what felt like fifteen or twenty minutes, but was likely closer to seconds, until the sound of the door opening pulled them apart, though not with a start as if being caught doing something taboo, more out of curiosity. Raina stared at them, a beer in each hand, a puzzled look on her face.

Asher brushed a few remaining tears from his eyes and smiled at his cousin. "I have something to tell you," he said with a shy smile.

She stepped toward them and handed each a beer.

"I think I'm gay," Asher continued, feeling his entire body blush as he did so.

A broad grin emerged on her face. "I always thought so, but the girlfriend threw me," she replied. "You like Larry?"

Asher shyly looked away as he nodded.

"He's a good guy," she offered, then pulled her cousin into a hug.

Asher had never spoken his truth out loud, deterred by shame and uncertainty. Yet, now, he found solace in them and imagined a path to happiness, an opportunity to break from some of the constraints he felt kept him down. If he would not let poverty limit him, he would not let fear do it either.

CHAPTER SEVENTEEN

ASHER SAT UNMOVING and silent in his cousin's car, looking out the window at the sad little house he shared with his mother. A shabby ghost of what his great-grandmother had left behind, its once bountiful flowers and lovingly tended trees and bushes gone to seed.

"Are you going to tell your mom?" Raina asked. Her eyes kept a tight watch on him, eager for a confident response.

He had not stopped smiling all morning—from the time he woke on her couch through the drive home. Not until they arrived in his driveway did the enthusiasm of the night before and of Larry's embrace vanish and the starkness of his life return.

How could he be "out" with both the uncertainty of his

family's response and the brutal legacy of Meade Donovan still freely bantered about in the halls of his high school? But, at the same time, wouldn't he feel more aggrieved by hiding the truth than embracing it, especially when he thought of Larry? "I will, in a few days," he responded. "I need to think about *how* first. I don't want to let her down. She's already been disappointed enough in her life."

Raina let out a sigh. "She'll be okay with it," she assured him. "You are the most important thing in her life. She'll support you on this."

He knew Raina understood his mother, but he still worried.

"First though, I'm tired of living in an ugly little house," he announced. "I'm going to do some work and fix it up. I might not make it as nice as when Nana lived here, but I can make it look better than this."

Raina smiled at him. "You go, boy," she cried out as he climbed from the car.

He had no memory of having lived anywhere nice as they had left his grandmother's well-tended farmhouse before he turned one. After that, they'd spent several years living in a decrepit one-bedroom trailer that sat on blocks at the edge of his great-grand-mother's lawn. Then, the summer before he entered the second grade, his great-grandmother had died. No one else in the family wanted the house, and at a hundred-years old and only eight hundred square feet, it held little value. So, the family gifted it to his mother—out of pity more than generosity. At least he finally had his own bedroom, tiny and musty-smelling both then and now.

The decade since his great-grandmother passed did not favor the property. First impressions would leave most thinking it sat abandoned, as only his regular mowing of the lawn kept any hint of civilization in its appearance.

"Hey, sweetie," his mother called out as he trotted up the porch steps. She kept the front door propped open, with only the screen door closed, to keep air moving through the house. An act that provided limited success, though not enough for most people's comfort.

"Hi, Mom," he quietly replied as he pulled the screen door open to step inside.

Bridget sat slouched back in one corner of the couch, a vodka-heavy screwdriver, obvious from the slight orange cloudiness in the clear liquor, already in her hand at only half past noon. "Did you have a good time with Raina for your birthday?" she asked.

Asher smiled and nodded. He wanted to say more, tell her about Larry, but now did not seem the right time. The dreamy look in her eyes kept him from it, as it seemed to impart a fragile happiness, one liable to break at the slightest disruption.

"I'm going to change and maybe work in the yard some today," he told her as he walked past the couch.

Her eyes turned up at him with a perplexing look. "Didn't you mow it two days ago?" she asked.

"Yes, but I want to do more, pick up the old junk laying around out there and pull the weeds out of Nana's flowerbeds," he explained.

A smile crossed her face. "That sounds really nice. Let me know if I can help," she offered, though in a way that lacked enthusiasm.

Even if her offer to help held little promise of action to back it up, he appreciated her making it. But more than that, he appreciated the smile he brought to her face. After all, she must think about their dismal little house too, run-down and serving as a public symbol of her failures and mistakes. He turned back to the couch and bent to kiss her forehead.

"I'm so proud of you," she said as she looked up at him, drink in hand. He knew she meant it.

"There's something for your birthday on your bed," she called out as he left the living room behind on the way to his bedroom.

A plastic shopping bag sat in the middle of his neatly made bed, a housekeeping action he did every day after waking, as he made an effort to keep his room clean and organized. The bag came from the same store where he and Raina got the underwear the previous day. He dropped his backpack and picked up the plastic bag. Inside, he found two shirts and a pair of shorts, all new with the tags still on them. Years had passed since his mom purchased him legitimately new clothes, as opposed to bags full of used stuff. He held up one of the shirts to give it a better look. A name brand

and stylish at the same time, not to mention the same slim fit of the shirt Raina bought him the previous day. They must have talked, Raina telling his mom where to get them and also the style and sizes so they would fit him in a similar way.

"Thank you, Mom. I really like them," he yelled out, not wanting to see her face as he said it because it might embarrass her.

"You're welcome, honey," she called back.

The total cost only came to around forty-five dollars for both shirts and the shorts, but any amount less than that had seemed almost unthinkable for them in the past. Maybe she got a raise? But through his open bedroom door he could see the top of the refrigerator where she always kept two cartons of cigarettes, and today he only saw a few packs. She either cut out or cut down on her cigarettes for a couple weeks to buy him something new. She'd sacrificed one of her few pleasures to get gifts for him, something he tried to avoid making her do as he knew how few enjoyments she had.

He pulled the clothes Raina gave him out of his backpack and carefully folded them to put them away, along with the new ones from his mom. In a closet full of dingy old rags, these would get his best treatment. Then he grabbed his toothbrush, deodorant, and new cologne and took them to the bathroom. As he put his toiletries in their proper places—for him everything had a proper place—in the small vanity, he caught a glimpse of his smile in the mirror. He had not realized he was smiling until he saw it—a smile held over from the happiness of the night prior. He also noted the slight stubble on his upper lip and chin, which let him know that he needed to shave again sometime in the next few days to keep from reverting to his rougher self.

Life did not seem as uphill right now. He took a confident breath and stepped a little to the left, but farther than he meant to, and bypassed the strength of the floor joist as he did so. His foot tore through the old linoleum, but did not stop there and crashed down through the rotted subfloor beneath it. A surprised scream escaped him as he tumbled onto the floor, his left foot and leg disappearing into the crawlspace beneath the house.

"What happened?" Bridget cried out as she came running through the kitchen toward him.

He tried to speak but couldn't make his lips move, even as his mother hurried near him. "Stop!" He finally managed to get out, and she halted right at the doorway. "I fell through the floor. More weight might make it worse."

Bridget nervously looked around, wanting to help, but unsure of what to do. "Do I need to call the ambulance?" she asked.

Asher placed his hands on spots on the floor where he knew the floor joists ran and positioned the knee of his free leg to give himself leverage to lift the other leg out of the hole. Up he rose, his leg easily pulled from the crawl space. Once standing, he grabbed hold of the vanity to regain his balance. For the first few seconds, both legs felt fine, but then they began to tremble as if ready to collapse beneath him. "I need to get out of here," he warned his mom before taking a couple of quick, yet timid steps along where the joists ran out the bathroom door and onto the kitchen's solid floor. The trembling continued a few seconds more with the thought of going back into the bathroom triggering anxiety. He glanced down at the leg that had broken through the floor, spotting only one injury, a small cut with a trickle of blood running down to his sock.

"I'll get that," Bridget told him, rushing to grab a paper towel from the roll on the kitchen counter. "That bathroom. I should have fixed it a long time ago. Now look what happened." Tears shone in her eyes as she dabbed at his injury with the paper towel.

"It's all right. I'll ask Uncle Roland if he can help with it," he told her.

A sigh escaped her. She hated asking her brother for help.

"It'll be good. He can teach me how to fix stuff," Asher continued, trying to give it a positive spin.

Bridget nodded, though resentment showed in her eyes and tense smile.

The bathroom floor might have a hole in it, but he could still work in the yard, Asher thought as he trotted down the porch steps half an hour later. He dropped onto his knees beside one of the flowerbeds that hugged the front of the house. The brick-edged planter contained not a single bloom, outside of a few late summer dandelions, within its weed-choked walls. He reached in with both hands and grabbed hold, the roots pulling easily free, then he tossed the vagrant greenery onto a pile beside him. Only the cheerfully yellow dandelions fought back, with their deep roots resisting. But with a little digging, even they gave way. He left only the thick green blades of the irises, though none held blooms currently, as he knew the next spring their vivid yellow and purple flowers would return. They were survivors in the face of his mother's apathy toward gardening, and he suspected that throughout his life they would always remind him of his childhood home.

The two beds along the porch quickly weeded, he moved on to the large round flowerbed, also edged in brick, that sat left of the walkway between the house and the street. Even the dandelions had abandoned this one with not a single hint of color outside of the unkempt mass of a white rosebush that sat dead center. A living relic in a field of swaying weeds. The hardware store on the square always offered a selection of annuals and perennials. He could buy some to fill out the four-foot perimeter that encircled the roses, but that cost money—money out of his pocket that would go to waste if he went to college and care of the yard reverted to his mother.

A hint of frustration took hold, and he kicked at one of the bricks, which were laid in an upright diagonal pattern around the edge of the bed, popping it loose. No mortar held them together, making his next decision easy. He pushed the neighbor's borrowed wheelbarrow near and began pulling out the old bricks and stacking them in it. This flowerbed, once his great-grandmother's pride and joy that had overflowed with a multicolored carpet of pansies, would be lost except for the rosebush that he would trim to a less domineering size.

"How's it going?" his mother called from the porch, a drink in her hand.

Only half the bricks had been taken out, the weeds still needed pulling, and the ground required leveling to bring it down to the height of the surrounding lawn. "It's going all right," he called back, trying to ignore the actual amount of work still before him. "I'm taking this flower bed out. The only thing in it is the rose bush."

She stepped down the porch steps and walked toward him. "Leave the roses," she said. "They've been here as long as I can remember."

Asher smiled at her. "I'm leaving them, but I'm going to trim them back," he replied. He bent, pulled up three more bricks, and tossed them into the wheelbarrow, all while watching as his mother strolled around the edge of the flowerbed, her gaze drifting across the yard.

"Nana spent hours out here," she remarked. "In the summer, she came out every day and worked for hours. I wish doing that could make me..." She started but did not finish the thought.

Two more bricks dropped into the wheelbarrow, each making a loud clang. *Could spending a couple hours working in a garden every day make me happy?* Asher wondered. Maybe. He could grow flowers, shrubs, and rows of vegetables like his grandmother did out at the farm. Yes, happiness could come from growing plants, or at least some measure of it. Maybe even for his mother, if the bitterness she felt toward life did not limit her ability to see joy in simplicity.

"I'm also going to trim back the azalea bushes and cut down those three dead trees," he explained as he motioned to a clump of leafless peach trees near where his childhood trailer once stood. "The neighbor's letting me use their electric trimmer and chainsaw."

Bridget hurried toward him, her drink sloshing and concern on her face. "Chainsaws are dangerous. I don't want you doing that," she warned him.

He shook his head. "I've helped Uncle Roland cut wood dozens of times, using his chainsaw, which is bigger than this one, so I'll be fine," he countered.

"I didn't know that," she said, then began to drift away. Her eyes glossed over, as if lost in a fog, as she softly stepped around the yard. "Where's all the stuff?" his mother asked, her voice slightly distant.

He turned around and saw her sitting on the porch steps. "What stuff?" he asked.

She waved her hand around the yard. "There was an old metal jack or something by the tree, then cement blocks over by the fence," she explained while pointing to the rusted chain-link fence that separated their property from the neighbor's.

"Back by the shed," he answered, thumbing in that direction. "I'm going to have R.J. come over, and we'll haul it off in his truck."

A distracted look appeared on her face as she glanced around the yard. "Are you doing anything to the house?" she asked after a couple minutes of silence.

Most of the large flowerbed was gone and the ground leveled now, only four or five feet of the edge remained. He would buy grass seed to grow something there besides weeds. "I'm going to paint it," he told her.

She stood and walked up to the porch, where she caressed the peeling paint of the old clapboard siding. "Paint's expensive," she called back.

"Don't worry about that," he responded, though he did not know exactly how much he needed to spend to make it happen. "The neighbor let me borrow a scraper for it because I need to get as much old paint off as I can before I put on the new." She hated when he borrowed from his grandmother or uncle but never seemed to mind if it came from the neighbor.

"You don't like being poor," she remarked, now standing at the end of the porch, looking out at him.

"No one does," he answered as he watched a familiar blue Toyota park in front of the house. His mother waved at Blaine as he climbed out of his car, before she disappeared inside the house.

"Why are you doing all this?" Blaine asked as he walked across the yard toward Asher and the now nearly obliterated flower bed.

"Got tired of living in the ugliest house in town," Asher replied.

"This is White Oak City; there are much uglier houses here," Blaine countered.

Asher smiled in response; while his house was rough-looking, a few others did outdo it.

"How was the birthday celebration I wasn't invited to?" Blaine asked before sitting down in the grass a few feet from where Asher continued to work.

"Sorry about that. Raina took me to an eighteen plus club," he answered. "And it was great. Really great, and something happened last night."

Blaine leaned back on the grass, a serious look on his face as he watched his friend.

"I kissed someone," Asher continued, his voice slightly trembling.

"A girl?" Blaine responded, asking a question rather than making a pronouncement.

Asher let the shovel he was holding drop to the ground and looked off into the distance. How did he tell his oldest friend that he'd kissed a guy and did it only a few days after he almost kissed him? Of course, he would not admit the last part.

"A guy," Asher admitted, or rather it tumbled out of his mouth. He timidly looked back at his friend, who sat smiling.

"I've kind of thought you were into dudes, but then the Jessica thing happened, and I was so confused," Blaine explained.

"That was weird for me," Asher offered. "I don't know why I did that."

The sound from the television carried across the yard, so at least his mother had not heard what he said.

"How'd you know I was into guys?" Asher asked.

"Ever since junior high, all I've talked about is girls, but you never do, so that's part of it," Blaine said. "And there's been a couple times I thought you were looking at me funny. But, it's cool, because I figure if you think I'm hot, the girls must too." The last comment he followed with a hearty laugh.

Both embarrassment and relief hit Asher at the same time, embarrassment for being as obvious as he had been, and relief for having a friend who seemed to understand and not judge him.

"You're the best friend I've ever had," Asher responded.

"I should be a better friend," Blaine countered. "That day at the diner, I should have sent Tommy to the floor."

Asher laughed. "Tommy's my problem, not yours," he said. "But, thank you."

CHAPTER EIGHTEEN

"THIS SHOULD HAVE been fixed a long time ago," Roland grumbled as he looked down at the sagging and punctured bathroom floor. "Why didn't you tell me how bad it had gotten?"

A legitimate question, Asher thought. He did not want to share the true answer—that his mother felt too ashamed to ask her own family for help. "I guess we didn't realize how unsafe it was," he lied but could tell his uncle did not believe him.

"Let's lay a couple of planks across the joists so we can walk in here. Then we'll pull out the toilet and cut out the subfloor," Roland instructed.

Logical and to the point—how his uncle always acted, the opposite of his mother. Nearly everything she tried was grounded in emotion and resulted in probably less than a 50 percent success rate. Asher hoped for a balance between the two in his life: able to make reasoned decisions, but without the aloofness of his uncle, and using his heart without becoming an entrapped victim like his mother.

"Here, Uncle Roland," Asher offered as he set two eight-by-twos across the bathroom floor.

"Thanks," Roland replied. He then handed Asher a wrench so he could begin to unbolt the toilet from the floor. "Raina said you had a good time with her on your birthday."

Asher smiled in response, though felt self-conscious about how much she might have shared with her father about what happened that night.

"I wish that girl would find a decent boy to settle down some," Roland continued. "She's twenty-three and always seems to have a new boyfriend when we see her. Her friend Larry is a good guy, but he's not into women so that doesn't do her any good."

The toilet popped loose, and a small gush of cold water came flooding out, splashing against Asher's leg. He shivered, but not from the water, instead from the mention of Larry's name.

"Watch your feet so you don't fall through again, and help me lift up the toilet," Roland instructed. "We'll set it in the kitchen for now. You met Larry, didn't you?"

She must have told him. She must have mentioned what happened. Her catching him kissing Larry on the porch and him admitting being gay. "I-I liked Larry," he replied.

His uncle smiled, not his most common expression. "You're young still, a lot to learn, but be honest with yourself," Roland stated, his serious look returning to his face.

"What does Grandma know about my birthday?" he asked his uncle.

"Grandma always knows everything," Roland answered before picking up his circular saw and stepping back into the bathroom. "She didn't need your birthday to learn anything new. Plug this in for me," he instructed as he handed the cord to Asher.

The saw started up with a loud whir, and Roland expertly edged it around the room, cutting through the rotted old floor. Asher expected a smell of fresh sawdust as his uncle completed the round, but instead it only seemed to intensify the mustiness.

"This isn't the first time this floor's been cut out," Roland offered once he finished with the saw. "There should have been an old board subfloor, but someone removed it and just slapped down a single layer of particle board. No wonder it sagged. When this stuff gets wet, it crumbles. And the toilet seal leaked, so that's probably where most of the water came from."

Roland then handed his hammer to Asher, instructing him to use its claw to pull loose the damaged floor. His uncle always had answers for the practical stuff, such as how to replace a rotted floor. He knew how to fix things and why they broke in the first place—a trait most would consider admirable, yet it irritated Bridget who felt it left her ignorant and rash in comparison.

The subfloor pulled easily away from the floor joists, with much of it disintegrating and falling into the crawl space beneath the house. What did not crumble only stayed intact from being stuck to the back of the of the linoleum.

"Why didn't they fix the floor the right way?" Asher asked his uncle.

"Lazy or didn't know what they were doing, and Nana wouldn't have known any better to tell them," he answered. "They're probably also the reason the toilet leaked. I doubt they used a new wax seal when they reset it."

The last of the old floor came out in a few chunks in Roland's hands. "I'm not going to replace the floor under the vanity though. That'd be a lot more work and the floor under it seems pretty solid."

"At least it wasn't Mom who messed it up," Asher commented though he felt guilty for saying it.

Roland dusted his hands free of the remaining crumbs of the old floor and turned to look at his nephew. "Your mom needs to listen to her own family more," he said.

"I know," Asher replied. He knew better than anyone that many of his mom's challenges came from the fact that she avoided asking for help. She would power through with poor decisions, even after recognizing they had gone wrong, if only to avoid giving others credit for being right. Where did that leave him? So far, dwelling in his own self-doubt, grabbing for confidence, but feeling it ebb when seeing his mother's life unravel. Poverty begets poverty, but not simply because of one generation lacking money. Instead, it erodes the positive influence of primary role models, one's own parents. His father had no spine, and his mother had collapsed into self-pity. It amazed him to think he could imagine going to college, at least when observing the past that had created him.

"It's creepy down there," Asher commented as he looked between the floor joists into the crawlspace.

"I wouldn't go wallowing around down there," Roland agreed. "Come outside and help me cut the plywood for the new subfloor."

Asher followed his uncle through the kitchen and out the back door to the temporary workshop, entirely comprised of a few sawhorses and his uncle's tools. Together, they lifted a sheet of plywood up onto the sawhorses. Then Asher stepped back and watched as his uncle measured out and marked it to size for the bathroom floor.

"Are you the one fixing up the yard?" his uncle asked.

"Yeah," Asher answered.

"Makes a difference," Roland told him. "A new coat of paint on the house, and it'll look like someone actually lives here."

A laugh, more ironic than not, escaped Asher. "Just because we're poor doesn't mean we have to look dirty," he replied.

Roland responded with a slow nod. "You shouldn't have to," he offered.

With a few cuts of the saw, Roland whittled the plywood down to size to cover the hole that was the bathroom floor.

"When I was real little, Nana still lived on the farm with us, but by the time your mom was born, she'd moved here," Roland said as he used his jigsaw to cut a hole in the plywood for the toilet drain. "She could have afforded a bigger house, but she didn't want to spend too much money. She lived in fear of another Great Depression, so she spent as little as possible. She also hid part of her money around the house, in case the bank went under. When she died, we found five hundred dollars hidden in her mattress, and it wouldn't surprise me if there weren't old coffee cans buried here in the yard with more in them."

They lifted the plywood off the sawhorses and carried it inside the house, angling it carefully through the kitchen and then down the hall to the bathroom. Roland then stepped across the floor joists, holding up his end of the plywood as he did so, and once he stepped inside the bathtub, together they carefully lowered the new floor into place, an almost perfect fit.

Asher cautiously stepped into the bathroom, feeling a firm floor beneath him for the first time in at least three years. He walked to the vanity, feeling no give, no sag, no more balancing on the joists, and hoping not to miss and fall through the floor. They should have asked Roland for help years earlier. Why did he let himself fall into his mother's rut, one of eschewing the generosity and help of their own family?

Roland passed a handful of nails to Asher, along with a hammer, and told him to start nailing the plywood down to the joists, a nail every foot or so. Asher watched as his uncle started on the nailing, to make sure he observed how to do it right, though he knew he would not be as fast. Not wanting to embarrass himself in front of his uncle, he cautiously noted the line where the joists ran and then slowly hammered away until the first nail came flush to the surface. He only managed about one nail driven for every four nails his uncle did, but he still felt proud in helping.

"Do you think that girl will be all right?" Roland asked as they stood together in the bathroom doorway, looking down at the new subfloor.

"I don't know," he answered though he had ruminated on the same question hundreds of times in the last few weeks.

"Her uncle's going to jail for a long time, it seems," his uncle remarked.

"Good," Asher replied.

CHAPTER NINETEEN

A RUSH OF anxiety always hit Asher whenever old Sam walked to the back of the kitchen. It did n0t happen often, but when it did, Sam usually started by staring at the teenager for a few moments before offering some gripe, typically a complaint of a plate making it through the washer dirty or that tables needed to be bussed in the dining room. Thus, seeing the stone-faced glare suddenly appear before him left Asher without breath and bracing for the moment's trivial insult.

"Your grandma's up front," Sam growled.

Asher stared at him in silence, expecting more to follow, but Sam offered nothing else, though he remained unmoving, his sour face glowering at the boy. "Can I go see her?" Asher finally asked, having decided Sam waited for him to do so.

The older man responded by shrugging his shoulders and walking back to his cash register.

Asher quickly loaded the dishwasher rack and started the machine, then hurried to the dining room, drying his hands on his apron as he did so.

His grandmother's familiar voice called out his name as he emerged from the kitchen. She sat, smiling broadly, at the lunch counter, with his cousin R.J. sitting beside her, noisily slurping his nearly empty soda through a straw. She spryly jumped down from her stool and hurried across the room to greet him.

"How are you, sweetheart?" she asked him, her smile remaining bright. Though he would not call her dour, she had never worn, at least in his life, the countenance of an ever-cheerful person, yet it seemed like nothing could sadden her at the moment.

"I'm all right," he replied, offering her a smile of his own.

She nodded in approval. "R.J. and I brought you a birthday gift, though it's now nearly a week late," she told him.

He could always count on a birthday gift from her but could scarcely remember getting one on time, so belated timing did not surprise him. "Thank you, Grandma," he offered.

"You haven't got it yet. It's outside," she countered, still smiling.

Outside? he wondered. *Why not bring it inside? Maybe a dog.* He used to beg for one until his mom firmly told him it would never happen. And now, with only a year of high school left, and the hope of college after that, a dog seemed irresponsible. He glanced around the restaurant and noted less than a half-dozen customers, none paying attention to him. Sally knew something though. Her face bore a suspicious look—a stifled grin—as she wiped down a table while not taking her eyes off him.

"Okay," he responded. "Sam, can I go outside for a minute?" he asked his boss.

Sam gave a noncommittal grunt.

R.J., with a wide grin on this face, rushed to lead the way, opening the door for both their grandmother and Asher to pass. Though the sun had dipped down behind the western block of the square, plenty of light still filled the sky at eight on the late July evening. Asher followed closely as his grandmother walked across the sidewalk to the curb while R.J. lingered back a few feet. He looked around, saw nothing obvious in the way of a birthday gift, and thought maybe his grandmother decided to pull her first prank on him.

"What do you think?" she asked Asher.

Again, he glanced up and down the sidewalk, hoping for a clue. Aside from the three of them, not a single person stood in view and no wrapped gifts or even boxes sat anywhere. Four cars lined the street in front of them—his cousin's truck, Sally's car, an old Buick, and a shiny red Ford Focus. His grandmother continued to watch him, the smile on her face growing wider, her left arm held out to her side as if pointing at something, specifically the red Ford.

"The car?" he asked.

"Yes," she replied.

No. "It's for me?" he questioned, though afraid of the answer.

"Yes, happy birthday," she said, followed by a pleased chuckle.

A car—his own car. Plenty of others at his high school had cars, many of them getting them as gifts on their sixteenth birthday, or earlier in a few cases. But he never imagined being given one himself. His mom could barely pay for her own, much less get him one, so he felt it could not happen till he could afford one himself. Yet here one sat, a gift from his grandmother. He felt warm tears building in his eyes. How could she do this? How could she love him this much?

"Thank you, Grandma," he managed, his voice wavering with emotion as he said it; then he bent down and hugged her. He could use his driver's license for actual driving, not just as an ID card. And it made so much more possible, such as a better job. He did not have to limit himself to working within walking distance. And he could drive to Larry's, so they could see each other on a regular basis.

"R.J., can you take a picture of Grandma and I with the car?" he asked while handing him his phone.

R.J. offered an appreciative laugh as he took the photo. "I don't blame you," he told him. "Now you can go live life a little."

"I wasn't expecting this. I can't believe it!" he told them. "Why did you do it?" he asked his grandmother.

She pulled him into a tight hug. "You deserve it," she replied. "And you'll need it, especially when you go to college."

College, of course. She always saw the brightest future for him. Even after Jessica, his grandmother still acted as his champion, urging him on and trying to fill in the gaps where his mother could not.

What about his mother? How would she take this? Would it antagonize her or cause guilt about not being able to buy him a car herself? Would it send her back into her dark isolation where she spent every night at the bar? He did not want that. He did not want it to cause her pain, but he also would not say no. He wanted this. He wanted the undeniable freedom a car brought to a teenager in a small rural town.

"She surprised you, didn't she?" R.J. asked as he walked the elderly woman toward his truck.

Asher smiled, an ecstatic feeling running through his body. "She did. She couldn't have given me a better gift," he gushed. Glancing back toward the diner, he saw Sam glaring out at them through the front window. "I better get back to work, so I can pay for gas," Asher told them.

His grandmother pulled the car keys out of her pocket. "That's right," she responded as she handed the keys to him. "I'll pay for the insurance as long as you're in school, including college. But you better finish."

So much faith. She never doubted he would find success in his life, and she always tried to help it along. "Thank you," he again called out to her as he watched R.J.'s truck pull away from the curb. He stood there a moment more until they disappeared around the corner.

"What was that all about?" Sally asked, a knowing smile on her face, when Asher stepped back inside the diner.

He held up his hand with the car key dangling from his index finger. "My grandma bought me a car for my birthday," he eagerly told her.

An excited yip escaped her. "Look at you, big roller!" she exclaimed.

"I can't believe it. I didn't ask for one," he explained.

"Maybe not, but you need one all the same," she offered.

Sam scoffed in the background. "Doing any more work tonight?" he gruffly called out.

They both turned in his direction, with Sally sneering as she did so, though Asher felt it risky for him to do the same. "I'm going back to work now," he apologetically announced. "Thank you for letting me take a break, Sam," he offered in deference before disappearing back into the kitchen.

Once out of view of the boss, Asher pulled out his phone. "Guess what?" he messaged Larry.

"I'll need more than that," came a quick response.

"My grandma bought me a car," Asher told him, even quicker

in his reply. His fingers and legs grew jittery as he waited for Larry to respond, despite only a few seconds passing.

"That's awesome. Now you need to use it to come see me," Larry answered. "And where's a picture?"

Asher sent the photo of him and his grandmother beside the car. And yes, he could use it to go see Larry. In fact, he couldn't think of a better reason to use it.

The feeling of elation stayed with Asher the entire evening, even as he washed hundreds of plates and glasses, so that smile remained on his face as he stepped out the diner's front door once his shift ended. Sally waited for him, a cigarette loosely hanging from her mouth as she leaned back against her car. He offered her an excited wave as he rushed over to his own car. He had yet to open its door. She followed him to it, offering him the pleased maternal reaction he did not expect to get from his actual mom when she found out.

"Show me your new ride," she asked him once he finally popped open the red Ford's door.

"I haven't even sat in it yet," he admitted.

"Then jump in," she encouraged.

The symbolic new car scent hit his nose as he sat in the driver's seat, though he knew someone at the used car lot only sprayed it in from a can, as this car looked about five years old. But, even if used, he now had a new car, or new to him, as the phrase went. No more borrowing the neighbor's bicycle to buy groceries. He could drive there. He could drive anywhere. If the urge hit him, he could sit behind the wheel and take off, no destination in mind, randomly heading down whichever road appeared. Freedom—a car meant freedom, especially when living in White Oak City and having barely known an extra twenty dollars in his life.

"Where are you driving first?" Sally asked as she plopped down into the passenger seat, being careful to keep her lit cigarette outside of the car.

"Home, I guess," he replied with a smile. "After that, I can go anywhere, right?"

She nodded. "Away from here at any rate," she offered.

Away. Since around the time he turned twelve, no other direction had interested him more. "Yeah, away from here," he murmured. "Do you think my mom will be upset about the car?" he asked her after a quiet pause.

Sally sighed. "Why should she be upset?" she asked, though the preceding sigh betrayed her response.

"She gets upset, sometimes, when my grandma gives me stuff," he replied. "Especially stuff my mom can't afford."

Sally leaned out of the car to take a last drag off her cigarette, then dropped it on the asphalt street and crushed it out with her shoe. "Don't worry about that," she advised him. "You can't help that. And you need this car. When you go to college, how will you get there without a car? You need this, and don't let them upset you."

Across the street, the town square rested in the dark, with the lights off in most businesses surrounding it, and the few working streetlights producing only feeble illumination. A constant state of disrepair.

"I do worry," he said. "I don't want to hurt her, and I feel I constantly do. I had Uncle Roland help me fix the bathroom floor this week, and I know it bothered her. Even when I work in the yard, I wonder if I'm letting her down.

Sally shook her head. "That's on her, not you," she answered. "The bathroom needed to be fixed, so you got it fixed. The yard looked shabby, so you went out and tended it. You think about a problem and find a way to fix it. She finds a problem and enables it. Don't be beat down by her unhappiness. I don't mean for you to deliberately hurt her, but don't hide it when you're doing what's right. You have no reason to be ashamed of your grandma giving you this car."

He constantly worried about the future. Spontaneity only happened for him when well planned, thus it never came. Maybe he didn't live for the day because his mother constantly did, and thus she seldom thought about the impacts or worries of tomorrow.

"I'm heading home," Sally told him. "Daddy's probably driving the hubby up the wall, and if I'm not there to referee, they'll kill each other."

She climbed out of his car and then walked back and got into her own. He watched her drive off in front of the courthouse and up the hill toward her home. A two-minute drive and probably a five-minute walk. Alone now, sitting on the square on a Saturday night in his new car, he took a deep breath, the aerosol scent leaving him slightly lightheaded. *A car, his own car.* Hours earlier he would have considered it fantasy to imagine owning a car. But here he sat, in the driver's seat of a little red Ford. Did everyone feel as if they owned the world when they got a car, at least their first car?

The key turned and the engine started, not a stall or a grind, no rattling from under the hood, unlike his mom's car. "Where to?" he asked himself out loud, as if both a passenger in the back and a chauffeur up front occupied his mind. Home. He'd worked a nine-hour shift, so sleep did not feel unreasonable, but who could go home and rest right after getting their first car? He didn't want to impose on Larry, as they had yet to have an official first date, plus Larry had texted him a good night message thirty minutes earlier. He could try the bypass, the popular place for the teenagers of the county to hang out on a Saturday night, driving back and forth between the dollar store and fast food restaurants. On a busy night some sixty cars might be there, and a hundred or so teenagers, from the fourteen-year-old wannabes to the nineteen-year-old lingerers, with a few twenty-one-year-old losers who found themselves friends, only because they could supply minors with alcohol.

The thought of cruising the bypass seemed almost embarrassing, but the emotion he felt in having a new car overpowered it. He wanted to show it off, despite it not amounting to much compared to Tommy Summer's new pickup or the prom queen's BMW. His car, as much as their cars, deserved an initiation into the rituals of adolescence.

The bypass, which twenty-five years earlier robbed the town square of most of its businesses, bustled as it neared 11:00 p.m. on the last Saturday in July. Dozens of cars, most used and dented, cycled the usual route, with teenagers screaming at each other while hanging out of windows, and others loitering in the parking lots along the heavily traveled three-block stretch. Asher rolled down his windows and propped his left elbow up on the driver's door, looking around as he drove, spotting some familiar faces, most of whom seemed surprised to see him cruising in a car of his own.

He followed along in the parade of cars as it careened into the parking lot of the drive-in restaurant. But instead of following the loop around it and then back out onto the bypass, he pulled into a parking spot and ordered fries and a drink through the intercom.

"Asher Brock has a car," a friendly female voice called out. His classmate Lela, who worked as a teller at the bank, walked toward him.

"Yeah," he answered with a smile.

She stepped up to the driver's window. "Did you use that money from Mr. Summer for it?" she asked, obviously forgetting his irritation regarding the money.

"No," he grumbled back. "My grandma gave it to me for my birthday."

Her smile remained. "It's great," she said. "It's very Asher-like, practical, with just a little fun, that being the red."

He smiled in response. She never purposely meant to say anything that would hurt someone's feelings.

"Want to take me and a couple of the girls on the loop in a few minutes?" she asked. "We have my car, but we need to break in yours." Her smile widened.

"Of course," he answered and felt warm inside. Sure, cruising wasted gas and offered nothing of substance to someone's life, but hearing her ask made him feel as if a special door had opened and he'd joined some elusive club.

Lela winked at him and signaled five minutes with her hand before heading to her own car, where two other girls from his class gathered. A car obviously helped make you more popular.

The carhop, a younger girl from school, dropped off his fries and drink, though she seemed unaware of his new ride as she did it. Even the french fries now tasted better. How was it possible that a food he had eaten hundreds of times before was improved just by having it in his own car? What about the soda? He lifted the straw to his mouth, but before he could sip, a taunting voice interrupted.

"When'd you get a car, faggot?" Tommy Summer bellowed as loudly as he could without it being a full-on scream.

The illusion the car had built in Asher's mind melted away, leaving him feeling as vulnerable as the night Tommy beat him up at the bandstand. "Leave me alone, Tommy," Asher growled as he turned his head to look out the driver's side window. Tommy stood five feet away, with two other boys from school, neither of them the one who had commented on their shared father weeks earlier. Perhaps Tommy had exiled him because of his lapse into honesty.

"Why would I do that?" Tommy barked back. "Where'd you get this ugly piece of shit?"

The friendly chatter that had vibrated around the drive-in died away, the only sound being the oldies music playing on the restaurant's speakers. An anonymous voice in the crowd yelled out, "His dad gave it to him." The insult inspired a burst of laughter from the teenagers who gathered to watch the altercation, most in on the joke.

Tommy's face flared red in response, and he stomped up to the car, gripping the door's window frame until his knuckles turned white. "Where'd you get it?" he roared.

Asher knew how to hurt him the most: to claim that Tom Summer bought it for him. He also knew that lie would render Tommy irrational, likely spurring another attack, maybe one that would end worse than the previous. Plus, Asher did not want to give anyone the impression that he took anything from Tom Summer. "My grandmother gave it to me for my birthday," he firmly answered, looking Tommy in the eye as he did so.

The rage in Tommy's eyes faded, and his flushed skin paled. It seemed for a moment he really thought his father had bought a car for his bastard half brother. He let go of the car door and stepped back several feet, though his heavy breathing signaled a continued agitation.

"I'll write your name on the side of it, so everyone knows it's yours," Tommy then announced, a cocky smile on his face, and a key suddenly appeared in his hand, held between his thumb and index finger.

"Stop it, Tommy," Asher screamed as he jumped out of his car. "Don't you touch it."

Tommy took a step back, surprised by Asher's willingness to leave the safety of his car.

"Guess you didn't learn the last time," Tommy snarled as he stepped forward again and almost bumped into Asher as he did so.

Fear ran through Asher's body, fear of being hit by Tommy again, and fear from remembering when his head almost got slammed into the granite monument in the park. But he would not back down, despite his low odds in a fight between the two. "Leave me and my car alone," Asher growled.

Tommy shook his head. "First, I'm going to knock you to the ground, where you belong, then I'm going to write faggot right there," he said while pointing to the side of the car.

Asher took a deep breath and stepped forward, bumping against Tommy as he did so. "Leave me alone," Asher cried out again. But before he could say more, Tommy's fist slammed hard into his stomach. Asher felt the blast from the hit reverberate through his body all the way to his spine. A blast that sent him tumbling to the ground, panting for air. He closed his eyes for a moment, trying to steady himself, and when he reopened them saw Tommy nearing the car, the key still poking out from between his fingers.

"Stop," Asher called out, but his voice sounded more a wheeze than a demand. The rest of the teenagers watched but said nothing, their mouths agape. Tommy laughed.

A shuffle sounded behind Asher, people quickly moving around. Then a loud voice broke through. "Tommy Summer, what the hell are you doing?"

Asher managed to sit up and spotted a sheriff's department cruiser parked behind his own car with a uniformed deputy walking toward them.

"Nothing," Tommy muttered with a scowl, his hand dropping down as he tried to hide the key it held.

"Did you key that car?" the deputy barked.

"No," Tommy whined.

The deputy crouched low and inspected the side of the car, then stood. "Lucky for you," he warned. He then put a hand under Asher's arm and helped him stand.

"What did you do to this boy?" the deputy again questioned Tommy.

"He fell," Tommy lied.

"You want to press charges for assault?" the deputy asked as he looked to Asher.

Asher shook his head, unwilling to add to the animosity.

"Okay," the deputy mumbled. "Tommy Summer, I better never catch you here again. Go hang out somewhere else. And you—Brock, isn't it? Go on home for the night."

Tommy scowled and stomped back to his truck while Asher climbed into his car, where his soda sat, still untouched, along with his french fries, probably gone cold. As the crowd thinned, Lela walked back up to the window and looked inside.

"We'll go cruising some other night, okay?" she asked, offering a gentle smile.

He nodded and smiled back.

The excitement of the new car had dulled to a near normalcy, much sooner than he'd hoped. Why couldn't it have lasted a little longer? At least until the next day when he would have to tell his mother about it. Tommy stepped in and ruined it. He belittled this joy and tried to make it about himself and his own insecurities with his father—a father Asher did not want.

CHAPTER TWENTY

A FAINT MUSTINESS always clung to the town bandstand, though not as pungent as what hung in the air at his home during the humid months of the year. But despite the unpleasant odor, or maybe because of it, Asher found contentment in sitting alone in the bandstand, his affection for the shaded spot having recovered in the weeks since Tommy Summer assaulted him there. It had morphed from a hiding place to a foreboding corner, to a spot for reflection, all in the course of the summer, and seemed to mirror how his own confidence had shifted during those tumultuous months.

A place frozen in isolation, despite sitting in the middle of the park in the center of the town square, even at the busiest time on the busiest day, usually when the circuit court held session, no one walked the hundred or so feet from the courthouse steps to the relic that symbolized the hub of town. It sat neglected, with peeling paint and rotting wood, its prominent role in town life long since passed. Decades earlier, a town band performed on Sunday afternoons with crowds of people stretching out on blankets enjoying picnic lunches beneath the shade trees, mostly elms, long ago destroyed by disease. None of his knowledge of that time came from personal recollection, though, but from the stories of his grandmother and others of her generation, those who remembered a more bucolic time in local history.

He spotted Jessica turning the corner opposite the old bank, walking from the direction of the old high school. They could have met there, on the front steps like last time. But in the glare of an August early afternoon sun, he preferred shade and hopefully a breeze. She offered a slight wave as she started toward him on the path that cut across the center of the park. He waved back.

"I heard you got a car," she said as she climbed the four steps up onto the bandstand.

"My grandma got it for me," he replied. "But it pissed my mom off."

She smiled. "Good," she said.

What did that mean? he wondered. Of course, after the summer Jessica had endured with her mother acting dismissive of her uncle's abuse, perhaps any slight against a mother felt warranted.

"How've you been?" he asked.

"I'm good," she answered, then sat on the bench beside him. "I'm moving."

The news did not surprise him as weeks of rumors among the town's teenagers left him expecting it.

"Where to?" he asked.

She sighed. "Joplin. I'm going to live with my dad's mom," she replied.

"What's she like?" he asked.

Jessica shrugged her shoulders. "I haven't seen her much since I was five," she answered. "My mom and her didn't get along."

Asher's own paternal grandmother still lived in White Oak City, and he occasionally caught her staring at him. She was a small, nervous woman who lived alone in a house up on the hill behind the old bank. She never spoke to him, as if warned not to do so, but when she watched him, he felt sadness radiate from her. Whether the sadness was for her son's public disgrace, or for her inability to know her grandson, he was not certain.

"My uncle will probably never get out of jail," Jessica explained. "They found pictures on his computer—pictures of other girls. I don't know how I feel. Part of me is relieved it wasn't only me, which is selfish, and the other part makes me think if I had told someone a long time ago, he might have been stopped sooner." Tears filled her eyes and trickled down her face.

"Stop it," he said gently. "You're not to blame for this. He started when you were a little kid. You had no control."

She shook her head. "I should have told you the truth when I knew I was pregnant," she continued.

"It's okay, and I have something I should have told you too," he offered. Time felt right to tell her. To share his own bit of dishonesty, something he might be too afraid to say otherwise.

"I'm gay," he then revealed.

"But, we..." she started.

"Yeah, and it's not that I didn't like it, but maybe it didn't feel right," he offered in explanation.

"I never thought about you being gay," she replied, her voice almost chipper. "But I didn't really think about you when we did it. I know that sounds mean, but I always wanted it to be about me."

They sat silent for a moment, staring off across the park, he at the boarded up former hotel and her someplace more distant.

"Have you done anything with a guy?" she asked, breaking their quiet moment.

"Just kissed," he replied.

"Are you sure you're gay?" she questioned.

He nodded vigorously. "I have no doubts," he told her.

She slipped her arms around him and hugged him tight. "I'm happy for you," she offered. "As long as you're happy."

A laugh escaped him. "Getting there," he said. "A car helps, so I can drive to Springfield to see him."

Again, they grew quiet. This he missed about their friendship before they dated. They could chat about almost anything, and when they finished, just relax and not say a word until some random topic popped up between them.

"Where do you think we'll be in ten years?" she asked him.

Ten years, everything in the world could change in ten years. What could twenty-eight possibly be for him? Hopefully, he'd have a college degree, someone to love, a decent job, not worrying about there being enough food to eat. Also, no White Oak City, no living with his mom, not regularly seeing his grandma. It meant his whole life so far would vanish, at least from everyday view, replaced as somewhere visited, not lived in, somewhere he told people about, but might not show them. Maybe that sacrifice—sacrificing his own background and upbringing—might bring stability, a bland ordinary life where he did not need to dig through the cushions of the sofa to find spare change to buy a couple packages of ramen noodles at the grocery store.

"Not here. I think I know that," he answered.

"Me either, but I won't be here next week," Jessica replied. "Where's your car?"

He pointed to the small red car parked along the north side of the park, across the street from the courthouse.

"Can you take me someplace?" she asked.

"Sure. Where to?" he replied with a smile.

"Not far. I'll give you directions as we go," she told him.

The new car scent had disappeared in the short time since his grandmother had given him the Ford so that it now smelled of nothing. A stale vacuum of being clean and unadorned. They turned east off the square and drove by the old high school, gothic and empty, then down the highway through the countryside, passing the cemetery where his grandfather rested.

"Take a right at the next road," she instructed, giving him enough direction so he knew the destination.

"Why are we going there?" he asked.

She did not answer.

The gravel road turned to dirt, then near a clump of trees he spotted the rutted-out driveway. He turned right onto the overgrown lane and drove slowly, taking each bump as easy as possible so as not to damage the car. On the shady side of the old house, stunted grass grew, so he pulled the car to a stop there, looking through the windshield at the leaning structure and spotting the broken porch railing still laying on the ground where Jessica had fallen. She opened her door and climbed out, taking a few slow steps away from the car.

"Are you sure you want to be here?" he asked as he joined her beside the physical remnants of her accident.

"My life changed, right there," she said as she pointed to the scattering of smashed banisters and rail.

Asher did not speak but followed her gaze as she looked up at the gap along the porch from which she'd taken her fateful tumble. The thought of the night bubbled up in him as an overwhelming guilt. He could have prevented it, been more careful, grabbed hold of her to keep her from falling.

"I'm sorry I didn't stop it," he muttered.

Jessica shook her head and looked over at him, a smile on her face. "I'm glad it happened," she told him. "It was supposed to happen. I think it saved me. It meant I wouldn't have my uncle's baby. Now he's in jail, and I don't have to worry about him hurting me or anyone else."

How could a tragedy be a relief? But he did not deny the truth in what she said. Though a tinge of sorrow still hung in his thoughts, as the baby still might have been his.

They walked down the hill behind the house to where an old spring house once sat, but only a stone foundation and shallow well remained. Why had this building disappeared, yet the old house largely remained? Poor construction or a longer term of disuse?

"Tell me about him," she asked.

"Who?" Asher answered, his thoughts still on the ruins of the farmstead that surrounded them.

"The guy you kissed," she replied.

He sat down on one of the foundation stones. "Oh, Larry," he said with a smile.

She nodded and sat on another of the rough-hewed blocks.

"He's in college in Springfield," he told her. "He's twenty-one but doesn't mind that I'm only eighteen, and he has a great smile. If you saw him without it, you wouldn't think he was super good-looking, but the moment he smiles, you completely change your mind."

A laugh escaped her. "You are super good-looking, so it doesn't surprise me that he is too," she offered.

His face felt warm with embarrassment. "He's a friend of my cousin's and came out with us for my birthday," he explained. "Later, while we talked on her porch, all I wanted to do was walk over to him and kiss him. So I did."

Another laugh, louder this time. "You player," she cried out.

He shook his head, embarrassed by the term. "Am not," he protested. "It felt right. I needed to do it. And when I did, it *was* right."

She sat for a few seconds then stood, leaving him sitting on his stone block, then walked out a few steps into a field of tall, long untended fescue grass, broken up only by pockets of purple-flowered thistles.

"I wonder if I'll ever experience that," she asked. "I feel ruined—damaged goods, that's what my mom said."

The words made Asher cringe. They were cold and full of malice—damaged goods—antiquated in use but still biting. How could her own mother disdain her so much? His mother had plenty of flaws, but she never purposely degraded him, never threw insults at him or questioned his character. Maybe, despite everything she lacked in parenting skills, her honest love and support for her son mattered more and helped him to develop the confidence to ache for something better in life.

"You will," he offered although he knew such a thought held no real promise.

He wished for something more profound to say, something about strength of character or potential waiting to be tapped, but it all seemed incomplete. He had no clue how her life would really go. There must be people who suffered similar traumas and overcame them, or at least managed some semblance of happiness in their lives. But he knew the opposite also happened, and he only had to look to his own mother to see that example—a woman so disappointed by life and the neglect of others that she collapsed into her failure. Surviving rather than living, grasping at life's basics instead of reaching for something more. And not money—he already suspected that a plump bank account did not always translate to happiness, though he did not doubt that a stable income could help. He saw something else as contributing more to his future happiness. Love, hopefully, and finding self-worth through a job or some other vocation, or having a family that made every day an accomplishment. That would matter more. He knew he could find it too.

Jessica smiled at him, though it seemed insincere, as if she did not really expect to have that in her life. She stepped back out of the fescue and took hold of his hand, leading him back up the hill to the car.

"I'm never coming here again," she announced, glancing down for a last time at the spot beside the porch.

"Me either," he told her. Why would he come back to some abandoned house in the middle of nowhere, a place only used, likely illegally, by teenagers on Saturday nights? He didn't enjoy those parties anyway, so any temptation to return escaped him. Especially with the memory of what happened here burned into his mind.

Neither of them spoke on the drive back to White Oak City, each silently watching the landscape as they passed—overgrown yards and empty poultry houses, decayed farmhouses and shabby mobile homes, all seeming desolate. Beauty did exist there as well though—rolling fields and wooded tracts, nature and country, the old stone church standing watch before the cemetery, a crisp white house, with a tall red barn behind it.

The car rounded a curve and descended into the broad valley that nestled the town. "Want me to take you home?" he asked.

"Yes," she whispered in answer, seeming to invoke dread for her destination.

Asher pulled the car up into the driveway and looked at the house, a 1970s ranch that once belonged to Jessica's grandparents. In the yard, he noticed a realty sign.

"It's being sold to pay for his attorney," she offered, disappointment darkening her face. "They owned it together, Mom and him, so she said he deserved his part of the money."

Still protecting her brother, even after it became undeniable that he'd molested her daughter.

"Where will your mom go?" Asher asked.

Jessica shrugged. "Rent something or buy a smaller house for herself," she answered. "She'll be alone, so she won't need much, I guess." In the front window, curtains fluttered as if someone stood there watching them.

"Are you going to have to come back for court?" he asked.

"They said probably not because of the pictures," she answered. "They said it should be enough, along with my written testimony, especially since I'm under eighteen."

"It would be pretty horrible to have to talk about it to a room of strangers, and him staring at you," he said.

"Yeah," she replied.

A moment passed, more silence between them. He knew she did not want to get out of the car, but he could think of no place else to take her.

"Maybe, when you go to college, I can come see you," she offered.

"That would be nice, though I still don't know if I'll be able to go," he told her.

"You will," she insisted. "Everyone knows you will. You're too smart not to go, and you work harder than anyone in our class."

All true. "College takes money, and I don't have any," he offered in protest.

"They have scholarships," she countered.

"That's what Mrs. Donovan says," he replied.

Jessica sighed, trying to gather the confidence she needed to get out of the car and go into the house.

"Do you want to go somewhere else?" he asked, unsure of where or what he could offer.

A big smile appeared on her face. "You care more about others than you do yourself," she told him.

He hated to let others down and sometimes went out of his way to help them if he could, but he never forgot about his own worries and tried not to let them get worse. Even when it came to his mom, like with the car. He knew it would bother her, but he kept it and told her about it, though his chest ached as he thought about it.

"I need to go inside," she said. "I see her behind the curtains, watching us and waiting for me. It's okay. I'll only be here three days, and then my grandmother is coming to pick me up and take me away to someplace new and a new school for my senior year. That's the scary part. I haven't been new at a school since kindergarten, and then it was here, so I already knew half the kids in the class."

His senior year would hold little change. He would go on till next May with many of the same students he had shared classrooms with since his second go-around in the first grade, eleven years earlier.

"Let me know if you need anything from me, before you go," he told her as she climbed out of the car.

"I will," she replied, and tears filled her eyes as she looked back at him through the open passenger side window. She smiled but could not hide her unhappiness.

He stayed parked and watched as she walked around the front of his car and then up to the front door. She turned back again and looked at him for a moment before lifting her right hand in a slight wave; then she slipped inside the house. If he had been straight, or if he had been into girls, could he have taken better care of her? Would he have noticed her pain? Had his own lack of interest and effort to blindly please made him apathetic to the torment that must have played out in her mind?

He backed slowly out of the driveway, leaving Jessica behind. Her escape from White Oak City would happen in a few days, while his had nearly a year to go. But he did not envy her.

What a day. The drive home would take less than five minutes, but he needed something to cheer him up before he got there, where only the television waited to keep him company. He pulled out his phone and scrolled through his recent calls, imagining his mother scolding him for being on his phone while driving.

"Hey, good-looking," Larry offered in greeting.

"Hi," Asher replied, suddenly feeling shy, despite having made the call.

"What are you up to?" Larry asked.

"I just left Jessica's house," he replied.

"Oh, what happened there?" Larry asked.

Asher sighed; he felt drained when it came to Jessica. "It's really sad, but I don't want to talk about it right now," he said.

"Fair enough. I know where I'm taking you for our date," Larry said in a cheerful tone.

"Where?" Asher asked, though the place itself felt completely unimportant, as long as they went together.

"That's a surprise, but I think you'll like it," he answered with a gentle laugh.

"As long as you're there, I know I will," Asher said.

"You keep charming me and you'll never get rid of me," Larry kidded him.

"So you know my plan," Asher countered, tempted to drive to Larry in Springfield right then, but also enjoying the anticipation of a real first date with him.

"It sounds suspiciously similar to mine," Larry replied. "And that makes me happy."

CHAPTER TWENTY-ONE

WALKING DOWN THE empty high school hallway, Asher felt the silent glare of thousands of eyes peering down at him from the old senior class portraits that hung high on the walls. His mother looked down from the class of 1992, as did his father, and then hundreds more, most of whom had never set foot inside the new building. In the old high school, his grandmother's picture had hung as part of the class of 1953, but only those from 1969 or later had made their way to the new school. Where did the older classes go? Stacked somewhere in storage or still hanging in the moldering second floor hallway of the old school? Surely the administration treated them better than that. Though, judging by the rot and disuse that infected the downtown, that type of callousness would not be surprising.

No bells, chatting, or rushing footsteps filled the school today, with the first day of class still weeks away. Even the hall lights remained off, and only a few echoing chirps of teachers preparing for the new year, and the grounds staff moving desks and furniture, met his ears. At the end of the hall, a glare of light shone out across the hallway's glossy tile floor, a beacon for Mrs. Donovan's classroom.

"There you are, on time as always," she called out as Asher walked into the room.

He glanced around. Nothing had changed since May—same desks, same posters on the wall, same comfortably middle-aged teacher leaning forward in her chair.

"I guess," he muttered.

"You are," she affirmed, then motioned for him to sit in a chair at the end of her large gray desk.

As he sat, he felt as if he came to disappoint her. He knew why she asked him to come, her continuing mission to motivate him and channel him into college. She had such expectations, the type he sometimes felt exceeded his capabilities. And she was not alone: Larry may have become an even greater proponent for him to go to college, offering his ear for Asher's concerns and insights on getting around most obstacles. To a degree, he knew they both were right, as he felt confident he could handle community college and could reasonably expect to secure enough scholarships to pay for it. But going beyond that seemed daunting.

He handed her the ten scholarship applications he'd filled out, most of them local awards, and none for more than $1,500 a semester. All amounts that, when combined with his lack of savings, still left him firmly in that community college pool, especially when considering living expenses.

"Are they all filled out?" she asked.

"Uh-huh," he answered. Filled out and he might manage to secure half of them. Then what? Student loans maybe. Those scared him, never having owned anything in his entire life and then taking on tens of thousands of dollars of debt for college, with no guarantee of a job or salary after the fact. How did this exist as the norm? Loading up naïve and green bumpkins with IOUs, and then expecting them to successfully pay it off. He'd read dozens of articles about student loans and the decades it often took to repay them.

"How about the admission applications?" she then asked.

"Yes," he responded. Before the last school year ended, she had given him five early applications to complete, most needing to be returned in the next few months, and all needing money included with them as application fees. Together, they would devour a big chunk of the money he'd saved all summer.

"I can't afford all the application fees," he told her.

"We can probably get a hardship waiver for some of them," she explained.

Hardship waiver, a nice way of saying too poor to pay, same as the free lunches he had eaten every school day since kindergarten. Two lanes existed for everything in life, one when you had money and one when you did not. Using a food stamp debit card at the grocery store, his health insurance being the state's program for low-income children, and a dozen other charitable resources that always embarrassed the receiver when mentioned out loud.

"Okay," he agreed.

Mrs. Donovan picked up the stack of applications and carefully flipped through, offering an occasional hum or sigh in reaction as she reviewed certain ones.

"You didn't fill this one out," she said as she handed one of the applications back.

He knew the one before it landed in his hand. The expensive private school, the one with an alumni list healthy with senators and governors. The best school in the state, at least for liberal arts. He glanced down at the application, which he had stopped filling out after his name and address. "I'm not good enough for it," he replied as he looked at it.

"You're brilliant, and you'd do well there," she countered.

Asher shook his head. "I mean I can't afford it," he argued. "I can't afford most of them. I only have nine hundred dollars saved from working all summer at the diner."

Her eyes narrowed. "You'll get scholarships; there are student loans," she explained.

"If I get every scholarship, I'd get seventy-five hundred a

semester," he responded. "Then, a couple of them I might be able to afford, but do you know what that school costs?"

They both knew the cost. A kingly forty thousand a year for tuition, books, and fees, and on-campus residence costs knocked it up an additional fifteen thousand.

"Federal student loans would help," she offered.

"Yeah, loans for a poor person," he countered.

"Stop that," she growled. "Have confidence in what you can do. And the university itself has need-based aid."

A bitter laugh escaped him. "Same as my free lunches here." He added with a scoff.

"You don't have to go there. Go to the University of Missouri. It's a good school," she told him. "But, with your brain, that expensive private school could give you a real leap forward."

Did it matter having some fancy pedigree school? It did. He knew it did, which was why the wealthy ran the world, sometimes for generations. How long had the first Vanderbilt or Rockefeller been in their graves, and their descendants still got Ivy League degrees? And how many generations of his family had never set foot in a college classroom, his cousin Raina the first to break that mold. Sure, he heard talk about college not being for everyone, how there was money for plumbers and carpenters and so forth, but maybe some of the poor wanted other options. How many Supreme Court Justices had children who worked as plumbers? Yes, working with your hands and having a trade were honorable jobs, and no one should be embarrassed to have them. But one never heard people telling the rich that their children should go to trade school—that was reserved for the working class and poor.

"Even MU is thirty-three thousand a year with the dorms," he offered.

"I know I can get you some help there, especially as our valedictorian," she told him.

"I'm not yet," he corrected.

"You could get all Bs this entire year and still get it," she replied with a smile.

Who knew the hapless Tom Summer could produce a child with an impressive IQ, especially when compared to Tommy's apparent lack of brainpower? Or did it come from his mother? Mrs. Donovan once remarked to him that Bridget Brock had been one of her brightest students two decades earlier. Disappointment in life manifested in many ways, not just emotionally, but intellectually, as a curious mind became less curious and interests less varied. He remembered his mom constantly reading, always a book by her bed and one on the coffee table. But, as her drinking and apathy increased, the books disappeared, and the television blared louder. Entertainment without thinking.

"How does eight thousand a year sound—tuition and living expenses?" Mrs. Donovan asked.

"It's a lot more than I have," he replied. "Where's that?"

She turned her computer monitor so it faced him. "University of Missouri in Columbia," she answered, showing him a page on the school's website that detailed its financial aid options. "They have several programs that would cover a lot of your tuition, then I figure you'll get at least half of the scholarships."

What about the other eight thousand a year? Ten times more than he'd managed to save working all summer at the diner? Then, pulling it together annually for the next three years, not including annual tuition increases? It really meant thirty-two thousand. Where would he get that much money? Outside of the account Tom Summer kept putting money in at the bank, anyway. An account created in Asher's name, but one he vowed to never use. A fund set aside to assuage a man's guilt for treating his second son as a nonentity for eighteen years. Why shouldn't he use it though? Did he not deserve it? Of course he did, but using it would symbolically give Tom Summer some sense of absolution—forgiveness he did not deserve.

"I heard Jessica moved," Mrs. Donovan remarked, bringing up a subject he found less comfortable than the one about paying for college.

"Yeah," he answered. His teacher knew the whole sordid story. Everyone in town knew the story. His girlfriend getting pregnant, him the assumed father, the accident, the revelation about her uncle's potential paternity, and the arrest.

"It's tough starting senior year at a new school, but it would be more unbearable for her here," she said.

Unbearable did not seem strong enough. He knew how unrelenting classmates could be, such as Tommy and his friends, when they found out something about someone that put them outside the norm. He knew the cruel remarks they would make, typically well away from a teacher's hearing. He had heard the word bastard at least once a week since junior high, as well as regular comments related to his mother being a drunk and promiscuous, with only the former having any truth to it. What slander would they have heaped on Jessica, someone who had already endured years of abuse at home?

Where did juvenile vitriol come from? Even he had taken part in it. The first day of freshman year he had sat in the all-school assembly making fun of a new student's name. He taunted him, and all because he did not clearly hear the name in the first place. And more than once in elementary school he accused other students of having lice, other poor kids, ones with more questionable hygiene than his own. His mother had always made sure he left the house clean, but their tragic home lives did not include that small assurance. In the years since, he occasionally thought about what he'd said and done, wondering if it all stemmed from his own insecurities, transferring the bullying he'd received to others.

"Did you talk to her before she left?" Mrs. Donovan asked, her eyes narrowed in a curious stare.

"She had me drive her to where the accident happened," he revealed.

Her features sagged, as if in contemplation of a heartbreaking sorrow. "What a tragic way to try to move on," she muttered.

"She told me it wasn't mine," he said, surprised he wanted to share that specific fact.

"You did not do anything wrong," the teacher replied. "You could have made a few smarter choices leading up to it. But I know you tried to support her when you thought it was your baby. More than your father ever did for your mother. I still remember all of that. Of course, Amanda Summer was the real villain. How she lives with herself, I don't know."

In two decades, would stories about him and Jessica still reverberate in the town, similar to that of his parents? Did they last forever, the juicy stories anyway? Like the story Sally had told him about his grandfather, murdering a man some seventy years ago, yet still remembered. Ugliness stuck around a lot longer than beauty.

"Is the reason you want me to go to college because of my mom?" he asked.

Her eyes grew wide in response, then narrowed as a smile came to her face. "I don't know for sure. Maybe," she admitted. "I see a lot of potential in you, and I did in her too. I feel that if you're not able to get out of here, get a decent start, I'll have wasted my career. I suppose it makes me someone with a savior complex."

A phrase he had not heard before. "What do you mean, savior complex?" he asked.

"A do-gooder, someone who goes around thinking other

people need them to step in and fix their lives," she explained. "I'm not intentionally trying to be that. I hope I'm encouraging you more than pushing you."

He knew exactly the type of person she meant; in fact, he could name three or four social workers who had come to his house over the years who had almost glowed with "savior complex." They rushed into the house as if they owned it and roundly criticized every aspect they could find, pointing out flaws or quirks that existed in most homes, and then declaring themselves experts on dealing with it. Typically, after these visits, his mother's drinking would increase in volume for a few days. One of these women spent three hours instructing his mother on how to properly clean the house, despite it being thoroughly cleaned the previous day by his grandmother. That woman had seemed almost insulted when she could not find readily available dust and had climbed up on a chair to point to a meager amount of residue on top of the refrigerator. She then wasted a bottle of his mother's vinegar demonstrating how to make a low-cost cleaner, a cleaner that left the entire house smelling of pickles until his mom threw it away a week later.

"That's not you, but there have been some of those who have come to my house," he replied. "I think they enjoy visiting poor people to tell them everything they're doing wrong."

Mrs. Donovan laughed. "It's not just the poor. They also love finding sinners. I've had several members of the local clergy give me insights on why my son is going to hell and what I did wrong that caused that—mainly that I got divorced in the first place followed by the fact that I didn't get married again."

Naturally, the local preachers thought Meade Donovan would go to hell. They thought all homosexuals went to hell, and if they heard about him, they would add him to the list. More gossip. People loved to talk about other people, trying to boost their own damaged egos by looking down on everyone around them. Maybe some people deserved it, those who acted without reason or purposely self-imploded. But why gossip about a high school kid, whether poor or gay, or both? Someone who burned through ten relationships in a single year set themselves up for some gossip; after all, one could commit to some self-control, but gossiping about unavoidable circumstances seemed shallow and opportunistic.

"Why do you stay here?" he asked her.

She sighed and leaned back in her chair. "It's my home," she told him.

Home. His, too, at least as far as background went, but it never gave him a feeling of warmth or happiness he imagined the idea of home should. "Even after everything happened with Meade?" he questioned.

Mrs. Donovan smiled, though not one of joy. "That hurt, I admit, but I've had a hundred good memories here for each of the bad," she told him. "I also have wonderful friends I could not imagine leaving behind. I don't think Meade still thinks of it as home, and that's painful to me, but that's because of the small minds of some people."

"I wish it felt like home for me, too, but it doesn't," he admitted. "It's more of a dead end, someplace I have to dig myself out of, not a place to stay."

The stack of applications still sat between them, taunting him, a possible answer to the dreadful scenario he just described. "How did you pay for college?" he asked.

"It cost less back then, and my parents saved a little money for me," she replied. "I also got married when I was in college, so we both worked and got by. Then I started teaching in Springfield and had Meade. When I divorced, I brought Meade back here and we lived with my parents until they died."

That divorce had created its own gossip. Everyone knew she had once been married, that Meade had a father somewhere, but no one knew for sure what had happened to him. "Why'd you get divorced?" Asher quietly asked.

The look on her face sharpened. "That's a bold question," she responded in a firm tone.

He nodded in agreement. She knew his story; why could he not find out a little about her?

"We were only married four years, and he didn't want the same things as me," she offered.

Asher kept quiet, though he wanted to know more, and stared at her like a dog begging for table scraps.

"He wanted to move off and live in a city, try to get rich, while

I wanted my son to grow up someplace more humble," she added after a pause.

"Did he move to a city and get rich?" he asked.

A broad smile grew across her face. "He moved to a city, but he never got rich, or at least hasn't yet," she offered. "He always had a scheme for making money, but they've never paid off. He used to call me asking for money, but I never sent it to him. He still occasionally calls Meade, but I think he gets the same answer from him as I always gave."

In some run-down urban apartment, the mysterious Mr. Donovan spent his days cooking up ways to get easy money, Asher imagined. Meanwhile, his ex-wife acted as mentor and patient ear for the students of a small-town high school. He could think of a dozen students and adults who would pay for this information, but he took it in good faith and would not circulate it out for others.

"I don't think there's such a thing as a happy family," he philosophized.

She smiled again. "There is," she countered. "I had one after I got rid of my husband. I don't think it's easy to have a happy family. You have to work at it, and if you're not working at it, you're probably being selfish."

He did not believe her. How much happiness could exist when all families seemed burdened by distrust or tragedy? He could not imagine his mother ever having been happy, not even as a girl, especially considering the way she complained about her mother and brother when they tried to help.

"I know mine hasn't been," he admitted.

"That's not your fault," she offered. "There's nothing you could have done to change any of that. Instead, learn from it. Then, as an adult, with adult relationships, maybe getting married, maybe having children, think about it and try to make the others in your life happy because I bet that will make you happy too."

Despite having reached the age of eighteen, and now considered "an adult," having adult relationships and children were daunting ideas. Could he find it someday—the type of relationship that eluded his mother? Living with a partner, sharing a life, holidays and trips together, visiting each other's families. And children? The traditional approach to attaining those might not work, but he had watched television shows and movies where gay couples adopted them, completing the twenty-first century version of the nuclear family. Could it happen? If he went to college and broke free of poverty, could he find happiness at home? The type of happiness that put family pictures on your desk at work and let you sacrifice style in life for comfort, because you did not need to impress anyone.

CHAPTER TWENTY-TWO

THE CAR SMELLED new again, despite nothing having changed about it in the last few weeks. To Asher, the excitement he felt the first time he'd climbed inside had returned, Tommy Summer's diminishment of it almost erased. He had driven it multiple times since his grandmother gifted the Ford to him but with only a utilitarian attitude. Tonight, he felt giddy to the point of bubbling from being inside his car. Maybe the idea of driving it to Springfield for the first time triggered that excitement, though it probably had more to do with why he headed there—to see Larry. Weeks after they'd first met, they would have an official first date. Anticipation left Asher increasingly distracted and self-doubting, regardless of their almost daily conversations on the phone. In his mind an actual date signified more than flirtation brought on by proximity or prolonged phone calls; it meant effort and desire.

The fields and farmhouses along the highway disappeared behind the horizon as housing developments and strip malls emerged. Outside White Oak City, Asher had spent more time in Springfield than any other single place. Even then, he only averaged seven or eight visits a year, less than once a month. Could someone have less experience seeing the world? Never had he set foot on an airplane or in a train, except for an amusement park steam engine. He could claim being on a boat on Table Rock Lake but counted the number of times doing that on his hands. Actually leaving the state of Missouri happened rarely, having crossed the state line into Arkansas a few dozen times and then taking a couple trips over to Kansas and Oklahoma. But by pure miles, he had never traveled farther than Kansas City, the Missouri side.

The lofty buildings of Missouri State University passed by to his left. Larry lived a few blocks from the college in a big old house carved up into apartments. Asher turned left onto a narrow residential street, once full of showplaces, but now many of the old homes looked shabby and run-down. His phone called out directions, bringing him to the front of a large brick American foursquare with a terracotta tile roof. Four cars crowded the driveway, so he parked in front of the house.

Time to go in. Asher focused his thinking, needing to boost his own confidence. He took a deep breath and climbed out of the car, feeling self-conscious and paranoid as he did so. Did the neighbors peer out of the windows of their homes to watch him? *No...no one cared.* And, if they did, what would they see? A teenager visiting a friend, going to dinner with a friend. Or would they instinctively judge him, some sodomite contributing to the decline of biblical morals?

He crossed the walkway and quickly stepped up onto a deep porch that ran the breadth of the house. A small callbox hung beside the door. He found Larry's name and pushed the button beside it. For a few seconds, nothing happened, further igniting his anxiety. Then the door buzzed, signaling him to go inside. The entry held remnants of a once formal foyer, now carved into an apartment house lobby, with a large and gracious staircase to the right, while the formerly cased openings on either side of the hall had been boxed in around dingy slab doors that served as the entrances for the first floor's two apartments. A shuffling noise came from the top of the stairs, and Larry's grinning face peered down at him.

"Come on up," Larry invited.

A jolt of nerves hit Asher, freezing his feet in place while he foolishly imagined being watched through the peepholes of the two doors between which he stood. With a deep breath, forcing an uneasy smile onto his face, he started up the stairs, moving at a cautious pace, though his heart beat quickly—one part of his body running while the other crawled.

Four steps from the top, he could clearly see Larry's blue eyes brimming with excitement. What was he supposed to do when he reached him? Hug him? Kiss him? Shake his hand? His right foot slowed to a stop on the second-floor landing with the left immediately following, and Larry standing two feet away. Asher restrained himself, for despite desiring to feel the warmth of Larry's body against his, he held back from offering an embrace and instead stretched out his hand in a formal manner. His smile unwavering, Larry shook his head, stepped forward, and wrapped his arms around Asher, giving him a quick kiss on the lips in the process.

"I'm glad you came," Larry offered as he turned to lead him across the landing into an apartment.

"Me too," Asher replied, feeling shy and not sure of what to say. He glanced around at the little apartment. The room they entered looked to have once been a bedroom before being turned into a living room, with a small kitchen filling what had probably started life as a sleeping porch at the rear of the house. On the wall opposite the kitchen, he looked down a short hallway, spotting a bathroom to the right and a bedroom at the front of the house, with windows that overlooked the street and Asher's car. The bed looked neatly made. In fact, the entire apartment had a tidy quality, despite most of the furnishings appearing at the far end of second hand.

"I like your apartment," he said.

Larry smiled. He smiled a lot. "It's big enough, and I can walk to class," he explained. "Not exactly one of these luxury apartments they keep building, but a lot less expensive." He put his arm around Asher's waist and led him over to sit on the sofa beside him.

"I made a reservation for dinner," Larry told him. "But it's not for another forty-five minutes because I wasn't sure how punctual you are."

Asher leaned against him on the sofa, soaking in his much-desired body warmth as he did so. "You said 7:00 p.m., so I got here at 7:00 p.m.," he replied.

"You got here at 6:45 p.m., and there's nothing wrong with that," Larry stated. "I have friends, your cousin for one, who I always expect to be thirty minutes late." He followed the comment with a laugh. "Want to show me your car?"

Back outside, Asher felt slightly more relaxed, especially as they neared his car. His shy manner evaporated as he gave Larry all the details, though most he had already told him weeks earlier on the phone. "It's not fancy, but having a car is special." Asher used as his finishing line, having exhausted his more substantive talking points.

"I know," Larry agreed. "My first car was a Dodge Neon, a birthday gift when I turned sixteen. I got into an accident and totaled it six months later."

The thought of wrecking a car after only six months seemed almost offensive to Asher, being so reckless with something that provided so much freedom. And seeming so nonchalant in mentioning it now. "That sounds horrible. What did you do then?" he responded.

Larry's gaze turned serious, and his smile faded, leaving him looking plain, though not unattractive. "I was lucky. My parents helped me get another one," he told him. "I know that might not happen for you."

Quite an understatement. There would be no second car, unless he could buy it himself. While Larry did seem to understand that Asher faced challenges, he didn't seem to get how daunting it actually felt. The same for Mrs. Donovan or Sally or even Tom Summer, who all wanted to help but did not actually understand how a day in his life felt, how draining the constant challenges felt. Why did he agree to the date? Sure, he liked Larry. They had talked every day for the last three weeks, but now he felt uncomfortable.

"It won't always be so hard," Larry assured him.

"How do you know?" Asher asked, his voice terse.

"Life will be easier," Larry promised. "I mean, it'll still have hard parts. So far, your life has been harder than most, but it won't always be that way."

Another do-gooder giving him advice in the form of platitudes. Why did it always seem so patronizing to him? And he knew the speakers usually found some sort of personal solace in it. "I know," Asher responded, his tone still hard.

Larry placed a hand on Asher's arm, taking a firm but not aggressive hold. "I'm not trying to preach or say stupid stuff just to say stupid stuff. I really care about you," he told Asher. "I get excited every time I talk to you. And I want you to know your life is going to be awesome. Anyone as smart, hardworking, and caring as you are is going to be a magnet for wonderful things."

The hard, metaphoric shell Asher carried to protect himself from the turmoil that constantly swirled around his life grew slightly lighter. Did he really make someone else feel that way when he talked to them? His heart sped up again, not from nerves, but something more intoxicating revved it. "I hope so. I know I'm going to try to make it better," he replied. "A lot better than what it's been so far."

Larry's warm arms again wrapped around him as they stood exposed on the sidewalk in front of the house, cars passing by on the street beside them. Did Larry not see them, or did he not care? Larry's soft lips pressed against Asher's, but not in a quick peck, like at the top of the stairs, now with intention and passion. The concern of others watching them waned from Asher's thoughts, and the weight of his fear and oppression began to lift. Why did he let the opinions of others force him to struggle?

Walking into the restaurant thirty minutes later, Asher felt elated, a feeling of personal renaissance bubbling up in his mind. He wanted to no longer unduly bear the burdens of others—not his mother's, nor Tom Summer's, not anyone's. He still wanted to do right by those he cared about, but not to his own detriment. Why had it taken so long for this concept to take hold for him? Had he lived his life gullible or naïve, or just desperately willing to please?

They walked up to the hostess station hand in hand, an action that at this moment gave him strength. Larry told the hostess his name. A reservation for dinner, only the second time Asher could remember eating somewhere that required one, the first time being a few weeks previous, on his birthday.

"This is the fanciest restaurant I've ever been to," Asher whispered in Larry's ear as they followed the girl to their table.

Larry's eyes betrayed his surprise, and his mouth slightly parted, as if about to say, "Really?" He limited his reply to a smile, perhaps restraining a comment that might have come across as entitled. "We deserve to do it up nice, occasionally," he offered.

Asher smiled back. Even if Larry made a regular habit of eating in places that needed reservations for dinner, even for only two people, tonight he brought Asher. It mattered.

They sat down beside each other, not facing across the table, and the hostess handed each of them a menu. Not the laminated, sticky pages he scattered among the tables at the diner, but large, leather-covered menu books, with the name of the restaurant embossed in gold on the front. Asher opened his and felt his eyes glaze as he looked over the pages; a few of the options he knew, but plenty of others read as if written in an exotic foreign language.

"What's the difference between an heirloom tomato and a regular tomato?" he asked Larry in a hushed voice.

Another hint of surprise showed in Larry's eyes—possibly

shock at the bumpkin he found sitting beside him?

"You said your grandma has a big vegetable garden," Larry quietly offered. "And are her tomatoes big and oddly shaped and different colors?"

"No two look alike," Asher answered with a smile.

"Those are probably heirloom tomatoes," Larry explained. "While the others are the ones at the store, all round red globes with little variation among them."

Asher nodded in understanding. "Now why are the salads with 'heirloom' tomatoes twice as much as the ones with regular tomatoes?" he asked.

A jolly laugh erupted from Larry, loud enough that a few neighboring diners glanced over with fleeting interest. "I think they're trying to rip us off," he replied with a broad smile.

Asher dropped his gaze back to his menu, taking a surprisingly long time to identify the entrée column. The possible selections again left him overwhelmed. Two dozen options and maybe a quarter of them sounded familiar. "What type of restaurant is this?" he sheepishly asked.

"They call it an American gastropub," Larry answered with a slight roll of his eyes.

A tremor started in Asher's fingers and moved to his hands, causing the menu to shake as he held it. *Stop being a fool. Pick something, anything on the menu that looks familiar. It'll be fine.* But it did not feel fine, and his stomach grew queasy. Who did he think he was, someone with sophistication or worldly knowledge? He had neither. Why did he think he could ever leave White Oak City if he couldn't pull it together in a restaurant? He took a deep breath, letting his gaze rise above the menu to meet Larry's eyes for a second, then shyly dropped back to the pages of indecipherable eatables. Why had Larry brought him here when McDonalds would be more appropriate?

"You told me you like steak," Larry casually remarked.

Asher laid the open menu down on the table in front of him. "Yeah, but I never have it, except sometimes when my uncle grills," he admitted.

"You should try the ribeye. It's really good here," Larry recommended. "Maybe get steak fries with it. They're also good, as are the Brussels sprouts with bacon and a maple syrup glaze. It sounds a little weird, but I think you'll enjoy it." His suggestion came with a warm smile, one that said, "I understand."

How could he know? Was his anxiety over the menu that obvious? Did it matter? He helped, and he did it in a way that did not make Asher feel a complete fool or a child. Who would recommend Brussels sprouts with bacon and a maple syrup glaze to a child? He treated him like an adult, albeit one in need of a little guidance.

"I'll take your advice," Asher answered, trying to match the pure joy he saw in Larry's smile with his own.

Throughout dinner, they chatted about topics of substance but without risk, meaning nothing about the sensitive areas that dominated Asher's life, though he'd already shared plenty of those in the last few weeks over the phone. Polite dinner conversation, Asher thought. Knowing what to say and when to say it, without spoiling the pleasantness of a meal. His mother would discuss anything at any time, not so much out of lack of politeness, but weakness—a need to find confirmation or to share her disappointments. At most meals they shared together, he sat quietly, letting her vent, always hoping for a time when she did not feel the need to envelop him in her worries.

Larry paid the check, doing it in a sly way—while Asher went to the restroom. And though he did not admit it, Asher was relieved in how it happened, as the bill topped sixty dollars for the two of them. How could a couple of steak dinners cost so much? At the diner, a steak with fries and coleslaw ran fifteen dollars, being the second most expensive item on the dinner menu. Only the catfish and shrimp sampler cost more, at eighteen. He had never eaten either of them there.

"Since you bought dinner, can I at least get us ice cream or something?" Asher asked as they stepped out onto the sidewalk in front of the restaurant on a narrow street near Springfield's Park Central Square.

"I'd love that," Larry replied as he pointed to a well-lit storefront a block up the street from them. Larry again took Asher's hand, holding it firmly as they walked toward the ice cream shop, neither taking notice of any looks—good or bad—bystanders may have made.

A few minutes later, ice cream cones in hand, they sat together on a bench in the middle of the square. Larry attacked his dessert with a focused passion, licking rapidly and making sure to not lose a drop, despite the determination of his two scoops of pralines and cream to quickly melt in the nearly ninety-degree evening air. Asher, meanwhile, daintily ate at his salted caramel, the flavor a suggestion from Larry, and one he enjoyed. Alone at home, he might act more like Larry did now in eating such a treat, but following his amateurish behavior at the restaurant, he feared coming across as a complete slob.

"My mom told me when she was young her mother brought her here every Christmas to see the decorations," Asher remarked as he made a gesture toward the abandoned Heer's Department Store building, which stood across the street from them. "She said she brought me here when I was a baby, but I don't remember it."

Larry smiled, ice cream smeared across his upper lip. "We drove down from Bolivar to watch the Christmas parade here when I was a kid," he responded. "Did you ever come for that?"

Asher shook his head. He would love to watch a big Christmas parade in person. Nearly every year of his life he had gone to the White Oak City Christmas parade, and every year it disappointed him, seeming to degrade in quality from year to year. How many rusty pickup trucks stacked with bales of hay did one need to see, most of them representing the dozen or so churches that crowded Decatur County? A flavor for every whim, his grandmother told him in explaining the variety of denominations.

"I marched in it a couple of years, when I played in my high school band," Larry continued, his ice cream now down to the top of the cone.

"What did you play?" Asher asked.

"Saxophone, but I was terrible," Larry answered with a laugh.

"I wanted to play the trombone, probably because I saw it on a cartoon and thought it looked funny," Asher explained. "My mom couldn't afford to rent one, and she didn't want to ask my grandma to help." Most of his ice cream had melted, dripping over his hand and forming a puddle on the concrete under the bench.

"I'll rent you one," Larry offered, his smile wide and eyes teasing.

He would too; Asher could tell, at least if such a thing still held any interest. Luckily, it did not and had not for at least six years. He remembered a night of pleading with his mother to let him join the band, and her refusal, even anger, when he suggested asking his grandmother to help pay for it. Had that been the night he discovered how upset his mother became when his grandmother stepped in to help? She had helped many times before that night, but only after that argument did he notice how red his mother's face became when he suggested it.

"I'm sorry about earlier," Asher said.

The cone crunched in Larry's mouth as he bit into it. "Sorry about what?" he asked between bites.

"Being clueless in the restaurant," Asher replied. "I didn't know what half the stuff on the menu was. Outside of the diner and the White Oak City drive-in, I never eat at restaurants."

The last of the cone vanished into Larry's mouth. "I don't know what a lot of it is either, but I learn more every time I go out," he told him. "You will too."

Asher gently shook his head. "Why do you like me?" he asked. "Is it because I'm attractive? Some girls at school have made comments to me or flirted with me, but they don't know me. They just think I look pretty. And I don't think I look pretty."

Larry reached over and took the melted and mushy ice cream cone out of Asher's hand, tossing it in a trash can at the end of the bench after he did so. "First, you are more than pretty—you are handsome," he replied. "Second, you are so much more than that. You're brilliant, you read all the time, you ace science and math, you take school and doing well in it seriously. Plus, you're super nice and thoughtful, always asking how I'm doing and if my day went well. You genuinely care about what's going on with me. I don't care if you don't know what to order in some restaurant that has a menu full of words made up to sound bougie. I care that you constantly want to learn and be better. I care that when you look at the hard parts of your life, you don't let it pull you down, and that you want to have a better life than you've been given and be a better person. So yeah, you are very pretty, but you're also amazing. I think about you all the time and am going to do everything I can to see you at least once a week from now on, if not twice or more."

His words spilled out in a rush, with warm teary eyes, as that beautiful mouth spoke these elevating insights. No one had ever spoken so kindly to Asher, at least not for as long as he could remember. Someone understood him and his worries and fears. An unfamiliar ease came over him, relaxing the tension he carried, and the self-doubt, even down to his half-hearted attempt at eating ice cream. He looked into Larry's eyes, which shimmered yellow with the reflection of the streetlights against brimming tears. Larry leaned forward, placing an arm around Asher's shoulders, and their lips touched, first with a gentle caress, and then with vigor.

CHAPTER TWENTY-THREE

ASHER WAITED ON the corner, watching as Sally crossed the street and then disappeared among the trees on the opposite side of the courthouse. Work had finished and the diner's windows darkened for the evening, but he did not want to go home quite yet. He had nothing planned and had no energy for walking home to get his car. He did not want to talk to anyone, thus his decision to wait until Sally left before he trod up the granite steps of the courthouse and sat on the top riser, a spot offering a panoramic view of the square. With the sun sunk beneath the horizon, the temperature had dropped to an almost pleasant eighty-five degrees.

This night marked his last Sunday evening of work before the school year started. He would still have the job on Saturdays and three nights a week, just no more Sunday nights, as he needed some dedicated time for homework and unwinding. For most of the summer, he had not worked on Sundays, but that changed the first week of August as Sam's trust in him grew. But despite getting another day of work in, it also typically proved a waste of his time, with only six customers arriving in the last two hours tonight. It seemed to contradict old Sam's insistence on extending the day's closing time by an hour and a half to 9:30 p.m. People might hit up the drive-thru restaurants on the bypass that late at night, but not a greasy spoon on an empty square.

A three-minute walk would get him home, where he would find his mother on the sofa, drinking her vodka and watching television. She rarely went to the bar now, and he usually found contentment, if not happiness, in spending the time with her. But tonight, he felt tense, his muscles and bones vibrating beneath his skin, though he could think of no reason for it. He glanced around the square, spotting Tom Summer's pickup truck parked by the old hotel, but no sign of the man, thankfully. Asher pulled out his phone and texted "Hello" to Larry. A response came back quickly, "Hello," followed by a half dozen *x*'s and *o*'s. It helped calm his anxiety, so he leaned back and looked up at the tarnished ceiling of the courthouse's portico.

If he hadn't worked so late, he would have driven to Springfield, but he knew better than to go now, as he wouldn't arrive until ten fifteen, and Larry had to work at eight in the morning, not to mention tomorrow being his own first day of school. A phone call would help fill that void, just listening to the sound of his voice, regardless of the conversation.

"Hiya, handsome," Larry answered, sounding his typical cheerful self. Sometimes Asher wondered if Larry always felt as cheerful as he acted, or if he did it for others, to make them feel good. Regardless of why, right now it helped.

The conversation meandered from five to ten to twenty minutes with a natural ease. They made plans for a date the next Friday and possibly the Sunday after as well. They broached the subject of introducing Larry to Asher's mother, the thought of which gave Asher a nervous feeling.

"I'm worried you'll be disappointed when you meet her," Asher offered.

"I won't. I know she's had a hard life," Larry responded. "And I'm dating you, not her."

True, Asher thought. He opened his mouth to agree, but the sight of something lurking among the trees across the street in the park stopped him.

"You there?" Larry asked, as Asher's pause lasted longer than normal.

"Yeah, sorry. I thought I saw someone in the park," Asher answered.

"Are you at home?" Larry questioned.

"No, sitting on the steps of the courthouse," he replied.

"There's someone there. I saw them, but they're hiding behind a tree."

Half a face peered out from around the side of an old oak tree.

"Be careful," Larry warned Asher.

Asher moved the phone a few inches from his head.

"Who's there?" he yelled out. Larry's now raised voice again warned Asher. The shadows no longer moved, but he kept his eyes on the large tree that grew in the corner of the park. The pale flesh of a right arm flashed in the feeble glare of a streetlamp as the person shuffled back and forth behind the tree. "I see you there," Asher cried out.

A loud, almost malicious laugh responded.

"Tommy, is that you?" Asher asked. For a moment, the now exposed arm remained still, then the familiar face fully emerged from its shadowy shelter. "What do you want, Tommy?" Asher demanded.

Larry's voice grew louder on the phone, though Asher now held it too far from his ear to understand.

"What are you doing, faggot?" Tommy yelled, his voice slurred, likely from drinking at the end of the summer party Asher knew took place that night.

Asher placed his phone back against his ear. "It's Tommy," he told Larry.

"I heard. Go home so he doesn't hurt you," Larry warned him.

"I asked a question, faggot," Tommy screamed, now trotting

across the street toward the steps where Asher sat.

"Leave me alone, Tommy," Asher responded as he stood.

"Just run," Larry insisted through the phone.

"I'm going to teach you to go around claiming you're my dad's bastard," Tommy drunkenly declared as he reached the bottom of the steps. He stopped for a moment, looking up the twenty or so risers to where Asher stood. He swayed on his feet. An inebriated oaf intent on settling his mother's aged vendettas.

"I don't say anything about your dad," Asher countered. "I wish I didn't know him."

The remark inflamed Tommy, his face flushing bright red, and spurring him to charge up the steps. He made it halfway before his drunken feet stumbled, sending him tottering forward, his face hitting against one of the granite risers. He was still for a moment, his face remaining pressed against the step. Asher started toward him, concerned, but suddenly, Tommy's head flipped up and he clambered to his feet, though swaying worse than before and with blood dripping from his newly bent nose.

"You!" Tommy screamed as he rushed up the remaining steps. He grasped for Asher as he reached the top, but Asher jumped out of the way. "I'm going to hurt you bad," Tommy barked, a trickle of blood also coming from his mouth.

"Go home," Asher told him.

Tommy shook his head and lunged at Asher, this time grabbing hold of a leg and sending them both crashing down onto the portico's floor. He swung his fist, slamming against Asher's cheek. He felt as if the side of his face exploded, but he knew better. Asher tried to crawl away, but Tommy came tumbling after him, using his ample body to hold his half brother's slighter frame in place.

"Get off me," Asher cried out, but Tommy instead responded with a drunken laugh and swinging fists. Maybe half the hits landed against Asher's body, but he felt like they were baseballs pelting against his head, arms, and torso. Tommy clumsily moved around, trying to get a better aim at his victim's face, but leaving his groin unprotected as he did so. Asher kicked hard, or as hard as he could while being pinned down by someone fifty pounds heavier. He had success when Tommy let out a howling scream and rolled off him into a fetal position near one of the columns.

Despite his head and body throbbing from the dozens of hits Tommy had delivered, Asher managed to pull himself up onto his hands and knees, taking a deep breath as he did so. A few feet away, Tommy continued to cradle his genitals as he muttered pained curses. An agonizing gasp escaped Asher as he pulled himself onto his feet. He needed to leave quickly, before Tommy regained his strength, but he needed his phone—he needed to talk to Larry. It had gone flying out of his hand when Tommy first knocked him down, so it could not be far. He glanced around the portico's floor and spotted it near the glass doors that led into the courthouse lobby. Pain shot up his right side as he stepped forward, causing him to pause, but he knew he could not stop yet, so he rushed in a hobble toward the phone. A few more steps, then break for home, he told himself as he neared the doors, but then an arm wrapped around his neck and pulled him backward, while a fist punched into his lower back. Asher cried out in pain, begging Tommy to stop, but the bigger boy only laughed.

Tommy dragged him across the portico toward the steps with some unknown and cruel intention. Asher thrashed and pulled away, managing to escape Tommy's grasp, then swung his fist around as hard as he could, landing it firmly against Tommy's jaw. Tommy cried out and spit a spray of blood as he did so. Asher scrambled back to his feet and stepped backward, his legs wobbling. He knew he could not deliver another punch as strong as his last. He turned away, hoping for enough time to reach his phone and race for home, but he barely made a step before the weight of Tommy's body slammed against him. Again, they crashed against the stone floor. Tommy lay on top of Asher to keep him from getting up and returned to his pummeling, hitting harder with each cry of pain his prey uttered.

"Stop," a voice yelled, loud enough to pause the barrage of hits.

Asher turned his battered face to the side and saw Tom Summer running up the courthouse steps. "What are you doing, Tommy?" the older man screamed.

"What I need to," Tommy growled back before delivering a few more hits. Then Tom grabbed hold of his legitimate son, pulling the drunken, bloody teenager off Asher.

"What's wrong with you?" Tom yelled at the bigger boy. He then bent over Asher. "Are you okay?" he asked.

Pockets of pain welled all over Asher's face, arms, and chest, but he could tell nothing had been broken. He lifted himself into a sitting position, though his arms trembled as he did it. "I'm okay," he mumbled, feeling dazed. "Where's my phone?" he asked as he looked back toward the doors. Tom quickly walked over to pick it up, while Tommy leaned against one of the columns, his face still red with anger as he glared at his father.

"Here you go," Tom said as he handed the phone to Asher.

"Why? Why do you act this way?" Tom thundered as he turned to face Tommy, who remained sitting. "Trying to kill your own brother."

An unintelligible scream erupted from Tommy as he sprang up and lunged at his father, his eyes wide with rage and his hands and arms flailing. The two collided and together fell back, almost collapsing onto Asher, who had just managed to get back on his feet.

"I hate you," Tommy bellowed as his fist beat against his father's chest. But Tom pushed back harder, sending Tommy rolling over onto his back. The older man then pinned his son's arms to his chest. "Stop it," Tom demanded, and Tommy's childish outburst subsided into tears and angry mumblings.

What reason did he have to hate his father? Asher wondered as he watched them. He was living the life of the legitimate son, not the mistake. Not the boy who heard murmurs of gossip or self-righteous pity wherever he went. Yet, here Tommy exploded in fury at the man who attended his birthday parties and never missed being on the sidelines for his football games. Even Asher did not hate Tom Summer; he just didn't want him in his life.

The portico grew quiet as Tommy calmed—no more wriggling, no more screaming or cursing, only a cold look on his bloodied ·face. "He's not your son. I'm your son," he insisted.

Tom let go of his son's arms and shifted off him, then sat on the floor beside him instead. "You're both my sons," he replied.

"My mom said..." Tommy began, his features growing dark, but Tom cut him off. "Your mom needs to shut up," he told him.

Asher picked up his phone. The screen showed Larry still on the line. "Larry?" he asked.

"You're there. Are you okay?" Larry cried out.

"I'm... Yeah, I'm okay. I guess," Asher replied.

"I'm already on my way. I'll be there within thirty minutes," Larry told him. "I would have called 911, but didn't want to hang up on you."

"You're coming here?" Asher asked, his thoughts still dazed. "Why?" But he knew why.

"You got attacked. I'm on the highway now," Larry answered.

"Thank you," Asher said, tears trickling down his face. "I'm okay now, but thank you for coming to see me. I'm heading home now and will text you the address." He ended the call and glanced back toward Tom and Tommy, still huddled together on the ground. "I'm going home," he mumbled to them, then started down the steps.

"Wait," Tom called out, quickly climbing back to his feet to follow.

"Why?" Asher asked as he looked past the approaching Tom to where Tommy still sat, his face wearing the expression of a chastised child.

"I should have married your mom instead," Tom admitted.

"It doesn't matter now," Asher countered. The life it might have created seemed impossible to imagine—and unnecessary. Why dwell on the fantasy of what someone else's alternative decision may have created?

Tom did not respond at first, only continuing to follow Asher as he turned right at the side of the courthouse on his way home. "I want you to take the money," the man finally said. "But we need to go to the bank together and get my name off the account."

Asher stopped, and without looking back, waited for Tom to catch up with him. "Why should I?" he asked.

Tom slowly looked at the aged neighborhood around them, at the weathered and darkened houses, and the old tress that created a gloomy canopy along the street. "To get out of here, to go to college, to be successful," he told him.

The money held that promise. Asher knew that $30,000, in

addition to the scholarships Mrs. Donovan thought he could get, would just about cover four years at the University of Missouri. But what about his mother? She hated it when his grandmother spent fifty dollars on groceries for them, so how would she take it to know the man who had abandoned her funded her son's college education?

"I don't need your help," Asher barked back.

"I know. You'll survive, but take it anyway and make your life a little easier," Tom told him. "We do need to take care of it at the bank. I'm going to get divorced, and if my name is on that money, she'll try to take it. Just like she kept me from being your dad."

Coward, Asher thought as he heard the excuse. "That was your choice, not hers," he protested.

"It was—the easy choice," Tom agreed.

Tommy followed at a distance, lurking thirty feet back, glaring at them.

"Give it to him," Asher instructed while pointing in Tommy's direction.

"He's not going to college, and he'd waste it otherwise," Tom replied.

No one pretended Tommy Summer would go to college, except on a football scholarship. Even then, his laziness on the field quelled any serious interest.

"I should take your money and forgive you?" Asher asked.

"Keep hating me if you want—just take the money. Be better

than him," Tom offered while gesturing toward his other son.

A loud sigh escaped Asher. "I've never hated you. You have to know someone to hate them," he replied. "I've never known you."

Larry would arrive soon, likely currently speeding down the highway toward Asher to comfort and protect him. Something Tom Summer had not done until this night.

"Why were you here tonight?" Asher asked. "You showed up out of nowhere."

A slight smile appeared on Tom's face. "Some nights, when I know you're about to get off work, I come over and sit in my truck and watch you," he explained.

"Watch me?" Asher asked.

"To see how responsible you are, how decent you are, and how much better you are than I've ever been," Tom told him. "Tonight, I parked down by the hotel and watched you leave work, then walk over to the courthouse and sit on the top riser. I saw Tommy run up the steps and hit you, so I came to stop it."

Asher wanted to say thank you because he meant it. He knew Tommy would have kept hitting him, perhaps seriously injuring him if he hadn't been stopped. He thought for a moment. How could he say thank you without saying it? "I'll take the money," he offered in a harsh whisper. "But I don't want my mom to know about it."

A look of gratitude emerged on Tom's face. "Of course," he

told him. "I won't tell anyone."

Tommy had stopped following, instead, drunkenly stumbling off in the darkness.

"What about him?" Asher asked.

"What about Tommy?" Tom replied.

"I want him to leave me alone," Asher told him. "He says horrible things to me, and this is the second time this summer he's attacked me."

Tom nodded. "I understand," he said. "I can take care of that. I still have ways to keep him under control, and I will."

It sounded more hope than fact, but the only option that existed for now.

"And stop watching me," Asher told him. "You had an opportunity to be in my life, but you didn't take it, so stop watching from the sidelines. You can text me or say hi to me occasionally, but that's it. I don't want more. I may never want more."

The smile on Tom's face faded, replaced by a look of sorrow, but not the anguish of new or sudden loss; instead, the somber regret of recalling a tragedy long ago cemented. "I know," he muttered.

Without the quietest utterance of good night, Asher turned from him and started walking again. Onward to home, only a block more to go. He listened to hear if Tom continued to follow, but no footsteps sounded. The older man stood still, watching as his less favored son, the rejected second, left him behind. As he moved farther away, Asher was tempted to turn back to see if the older man continued to stand there, but it seemed disingenuous to offer the spark of hope that action might provide. He would see him the next week, anyway, to go to the bank and secure the money, the tens of thousands a guilty conscience amassed. After that, a relationship might exist between the two. A vague, infrequent communication that might ebb and flow over the next thirty or forty years, followed by back-row attendance at a sparse funeral with no mention in the obituary.

CHAPTER TWENTY-FOUR

"ASH," BRIDGET BROCK gasped out as her son stepped inside the front door. "What happened to you?" Her hands took hold of his arms, and she led him to the sofa, though her eyes never left his battered and bloody face. "Tell me what happened," she pleaded.

Asher dropped onto the sofa, his body aching as he did so. He leaned his head back and took a deep breath. "Tommy Summer beat me up," he offered in an exhausted voice.

"That little—" she started, before abruptly interrupting her own thought. "I'm taking you to the hospital."

He shook his head. "It's not bad," he protested.

Her eyes widened, signaling her disbelief. "You're so bloody," she cried.

"My nose," he explained. "Can I have a washcloth?"

She silently gazed at him for a moment before rushing to the bathroom.

In ten minutes, Larry would arrive, and he would have to explain that to his mother as she fussed over his wounds. She had never played the part of the overprotective mother, except when he was physically hurt, and then she flew into Florence Nightingale mode.

Water ran in the bathroom, but he also heard her digging through drawers and cabinets, pulling together every first aid item in the house. On the coffee table, her bottle of vodka and a glass half full of her screwdriver sat while the television blared a generic reality show about a rich white woman. He hated those shows.

"Mom," he called out. The shuffling in the bathroom grew more hurried, followed by a rushed padding of bare feet across the kitchen linoleum floor.

"I'm here," she cried out as she returned to the living room, her arms heavy with bottles, bandages, and towels. She dropped her burden onto the coffee table, unsettling the vodka bottle, which Asher managed to steady with a pained stretch and grab. "Sit back now," she insisted.

A squeaky, fake posh accent emanated from the television as he closed his eyes and let his body ease into the old sofa, his head tilted slightly over the raised back.

"It's all my fault," she offered as she gently wiped the blood from his face. "I should have done more to protect you."

He opened his eyes to see tears trickling down her cheeks. "You tried," he told her, knowing the statement included some truth, but also wishing she had done more.

"You deserved better," she replied, tears now dripping from her chin. She picked up a dry towel and softly patted his bruised skin. "The only blood was from your nose, but I don't think it's broken."

Battered, but not broken; bruised, but not cut. He'd survived his second assault by Tommy Summer only a little worse off than the first.

"My father stopped it," he said.

"What?" she asked, as she carefully daubed arnica cream on his sore face.

"Tom Summer was there," Asher explained. "He saw Tommy attack me, then came and pulled him off me."

Neither spoke for a moment.

"Tommy said he hated him—hated his own dad," Asher continued. "He has a dad at home every night, but he hates him. Tom Summer never made a single effort to be in my life, but I don't hate him. I feel sorry for him for being weak, but I don't hate him."

Bridget handed him two ibuprofens. "I'm weak. I know I am," she said in a weary tone as she shook her head.

"You're not. You've just had a hard life," he argued. "You've tried to do everything you could for me. But it's not easy, especially living here."

A sob escaped her, and she put her right hand to her mouth to stifle another. "I am weak," she cried out. "I drink too much. I smoke too much. All that time I spend going to the bar instead of being home with you. Always looking for a man instead of raising one."

Despite the pain still throbbing through his body, Asher reached out and grabbed hold of his mother's arm, pulling her down onto the couch beside him. "You do take care of me," he countered. "We have a home; you get me what you can. I know that. I'm going to make you proud. I'm going to go to college, get a good job, and help take care of you."

She took his right hand into her left, and leaned against his shoulder. "You're going to do wonderful things in your life," she told him. "But do it for you, not me." A sniffle escaped her. "I should have let your grandma help more, and your uncle. They always tried, and I always pushed back. I felt ashamed. Now, I only have you for one more year, then off you'll go. I'm going to make you a promise. I'm not doing that anymore. If they want to help, I'll let them, and I'm not going back to the bar. I also need to stop drinking. I'll try to stop smoking, too, but that might be harder."

Every word came out in complete sincerity. He knew she meant it, even the alcohol and smoking. He felt in his gut that the nightly ritual of vodka and orange juice would disappear, at least while he still lived in the house. She would sacrifice her crutches and grudges for him. And he would let her do it, because they needed it. He needed to know that she would do anything for him, and she needed to reexperience having a child to care for and treasure.

"I thought our family was the only screwed up one," he said. "The other kids at school have married parents, nicer clothes, and bigger houses. I sometimes wished I was them. They all seem happy and don't worry about having food at home, holes in their clothes, or collapsing bathroom floors."

She sighed. "I gave you a worse life than I thought," she replied as she shook her head.

"That's not what I'm saying," he protested. "A lot of their lives suck too. Look at Jessica. Who knew her uncle did that to her? She always acted in control, even bossy. But she wasn't—she was being hurt. Yeah, maybe our house needs some work, and I don't have expensive clothes, but that's nothing compared to what happened to her. Her mother knew. But instead of blaming the uncle, she blamed her daughter. You never would have let that happen to me. You almost killed a guy who followed me into the bathroom."

She laughed now. "I should have killed him," she offered. "But I never should have brought a bunch of strange men over. Any of them could have hurt you."

He shook his head. "Anything can hurt me," he told her. "You raised me to pay attention and be aware. That's how you protected me from those people."

Back as far as his toddler years, she'd always warned him to pay attention to what went on around him, from cars on the road to people and stray animals. And she frequently reinforced that no one could make him do something he did not want to do. A learned trait that made him so willing to stand up to Tommy, even if he knew he would lose any fight between them.

"The Summers—they must be miserable," Asher continued. "Tommy got the dad, and he hates him. His mother sits there telling him all the reasons to hate me. What type of nasty person tells her child to hate another child? Tom Summer told me he watches me. He sits in his car after I get off work and watches me while I walk down the street. He's so unhappy with his own life that he makes believe he's part of mine. He made a choice, and eighteen years later, he still can't let go of it. His hopes and dreams are in me, not in the son he raised and lives with. That's why Tommy hates him so much. He feels stuck in some sort of competition with me for something I don't want. I told Tom tonight I don't need him in my life."

The plastic faces on the television yapped on, though the room seemed to grow silent. A serene look rested on his mother's face as through the screen door a car could be heard approaching.

"Families can be happy," she told him, breaking the quiet mood. "There are unhappy ones, but I think there are more of the other. I know you'll have a happy family because you'll make it one. You'll do everything you can, so it isn't like Jessica's or Tom's or us."

He wanted to protest, but how could he protest the truth? He wished he could say they had a happy family. But he could not lie to placate her. The happy moments or times he could remember seemed fleeting, occasional oases of joy among a desert of disappointment. If their unhappiness did not stem from his mother's discontented circumstances in life, it came from their poverty, failing to live paycheck to paycheck, surviving only by clinging to the stigma of food stamps and charity pantries.

How often had he seen the false happiness on the faces of those handing out grocery bags of expired canned goods when the kitchen stock and paycheck simultaneously evaporated? They smiled as if they were contestants in a beauty pageant, enthused but looking down on others with superiority. An experience he had found nearly identical in the hundreds of visits they made to food banks through the years, all the way back to him sitting in a stroller, watching a woman roll her eyes when his mother pointed out mold on a loaf of bread. That woman, with her false emotions, had let her façade slip and delivered an eye roll that said: "You're poor; deal with it." That produced a memory he would never scour from his brain.

Outside, a car door slammed.

"Someone's here," his mother noted.

"It's Larry," he replied.

The look on her faced showed familiarity rather than surprise.

The screen door rattled as Larry knocked on it. Wearing a serious look, he peered inside to where they sat on the sofa. Bridget jumped up and hurried to the door, unlatching it and pushing it open so he could come inside.

With unintentionally rude haste, Larry brushed past her in his dash to the sofa, where he leaned forward and took Asher's battered face in his hands. "My god, look at you," he cried out. "You're all bruised and swollen."

Tears burst from Asher's eyes. "I'm okay. My mom is taking care of me," he said, feeling a blooming warmth in his chest in response to the presence and soft touch of his new love.

Then, almost sheepishly, Larry turned back to face Bridget, who still stood near the door, a nervous look on her face. "Hi," he greeted. "I'm Larry, uh, a friend of Asher's."

She nodded. "I know," she replied. "Raina told me about you."

What had Raina told her? Asher wondered. His mind began racing with concern and a tinge of anger. What right did Raina have? This was his business, and he deserved to tell her when he felt ready. But when would that have happened? Every time he thought about it, he worried it would upset her. After Jessica, and the car, and Tom and Tommy, the events of this summer had upset her enough. Several opportunities to tell her had occurred, but right as he started to say something, he grew afraid, creating excuses to avoid doing it.

"What did Raina say?" Asher asked. He could tell by Larry's tightening grasp of his arm that he also wanted to know, though more out of curiosity than concern.

"That you met a friend of hers and became close to him," Bridget answered.

"Just friends?" Larry interjected, his charming smile finally appearing.

Bridget smiled in response, a knowing smile, one that showed her as much less naïve or blind to her son's life than he expected. "A bit more than that," she confessed.

"You mean, you know about me," Asher cautiously questioned.

"Yep," she answered as she walked around the coffee table to sit beside him, sandwiching him between her and Larry, who had also sat on the couch. "I've known since you were a little boy, or at least I suspected," she explained.

"What about Jessica?" he asked. After all, he'd spent three months of the last year with a girlfriend.

"She's more damaged than you are," she offered.

"I'm damaged?" he asked.

Her eyes narrowed as she looked at him, and he could feel Larry's hand taking hold of his own.

"A little," she answered. "You got beat up tonight by your own half brother. You've known your father your entire life, but he acted as if you didn't exist. You were told you were going to have a baby a couple months ago, but it wasn't yours. It was your girlfriend's uncle's baby. I think you might be a little damaged. But you're still smart, kind, and loving. You work hard and want a better life. Even if you have some damage, you're still wonderful."

Asher turned to look at Larry. "Evidently, I'm damaged," he said.

Larry shrugged his shoulders. "I don't mind," he replied.

The bruises still ached, but not with the pulsing sharpness he felt when he first collapsed on the sofa after staggering home from the courthouse. "I feel a little better now," he offered. "Can we go outside and sit on the porch? I know it's hot, but we don't have an air conditioner, so it's hot in here too."

Larry stood and put out his hand to help Asher onto his feet.

"Thank you," Asher said, accepting the help as he rose back to standing.

"You boys go out," Bridget told them, and then she, too, stood. "I'm going to clean up in here."

Using a gentle touch, Larry slid his arm around Asher's lower back and ushered him out through the front door. They could hear fluid being poured down the kitchen sink. It would only be temporary, his mother's abstinence from alcohol probably ending in less than a year. But long enough for her to enjoy the limited time she had left with a son at home. Once high school ended and he left for college and whatever followed, her self-destructive habits might return—evenings at the bar, a constant supply of cheap vodka in the fridge and a couple packs of Parliament Lights a day. Or maybe not—a year of clear-headed mornings might awake new confidence in her, help her build a quality life in knowing she did better for her son. Could he safeguard that type of future for her if he stayed? Unknowable, and he might risk losing himself if he tried.

"Want to sit here?" Larry asked, pointing to a pair of faded and peeling clamshell-back lawn chairs.

"Yeah, I just need to sit down slowly," he answered.

Larry kept hold of Asher's arm as he carefully lowered down into one of the chairs. He then sat next to him.

"How did you know where my house was?" Asher questioned, realizing he had forgotten to text the address.

A sly smile appeared on Larry's face. "I asked Raina for your address the day after our first date," he admitted, his smile growing to a broad grin.

"Raina's the center of the universe," Asher exclaimed.

"She is awfully involved," Larry agreed. "But not in a bad way. She doesn't criticize or complain. She tries to help."

Asher shrugged, trying to play it off with indifference, but he knew she cared, and always had. Despite being four years older than him, when they were children, she always involved him and played with him. She never treated him as an annoyance.

"Did you call the police?" Larry asked.

"Why?" Asher responded, having almost forgotten the fight.

"To get Tommy arrested," Larry urged, a hint of frustration in his voice.

"It doesn't matter," Asher told him, which he honestly believed.

"What if he does it again?" Larry protested.

Unlikely. The fight ended with Tom pushing Tommy off, and Tommy lashing out at his father. The emotion broke. It hit its peak. Tommy would never be friends with him. He would still glare at him in passing, but never again would he act the aggressor. Tom Summer broke that by acknowledging his paternity in front of both of his sons. All the anger that came from Tommy's denial of a fact that everyone knew had vanished. His own stability in his life might also vanish, as based on Tom Summer's remarks, divorce would soon come to that scarred family.

"It won't," Asher assured him, though he still saw doubt in Larry's eyes. "Did I tell you this house belonged to my great-grandmother?"

Larry shook his head.

"When she was alive, Mom and I lived in a trailer that sat over there," he explained while pointing across the porch to the empty expanse of yard to the north. "When she died, we moved into the house. It looked nicer then."

Did he need to say that? Deprecate his home. Always too self-critical, and how did that help? Working in the yard helped—cleaning it up, planting flowers, trimming bushes, getting rid of trash. That brought accomplishment and pride. Larry did not care if the house looked worse than when his great-grandmother lived in it. But he did care about what Asher did to improve it. He always asked for pictures of the work he did in the yard. That mattered, not the teardown.

"What was your great-grandmother like?" Larry asked.

"She always smiled at me," Asher replied. "She baked cookies for me. She would sit me on the couch to watch cartoons while she sat at her sewing machine. Whenever I looked up at her, she'd say, 'Hello, beautiful.'" The woman's wise and wrinkled face smiled back at him from these memories, a piece of his past that did not represent disappointment or sorrow, only kindness.

"Hello, beautiful," Larry now softly said, his blue eyes gazing deeply into his.

About Jeff Billington

Jeff Billington grew up on a farm in the Ozark Mountains of Southwest Missouri, surrounded by animals, family, and local lore. His adult life has included stints as a journalist, communications director for a member of Congress, and working for environmental and advocacy nonprofits. He currently lives in the Maryland suburbs of Washington, DC but hopes to return to the Ozarks someday.

Facebook

www.facebook.com/jeffbillingtonauthor

Twitter

@jeffbillington

Website

www.jeffbillington.com